DARK EBB
GRIM TALES

VOLUME 1

DARK EBB
GRIM TALES

VOLUME 1

LAUREL MCHARGUE

STRACK PRESS LLC | COLORADO

This is a work of fiction. All characters, places, and events portrayed in this book are the product of the author's imagination. Any resemblance to actual persons, living or dead, events, or locales is entirely coincidental.

Dark Ebb: Grim Tales
Volume 1

Published by Strack Press LLC
Salida, CO

FIRST EDITION 2020

Library of Congress Control Number: 2020932603
McHargue, Laurel, Author
Dark Ebb: Grim Tales
Laurel McHargue

ISBN: 978-1-9458370-1-2

Artwork by Laurel McHargue
Cover Design by Mercedes Piñera

PRINTED IN THE UNITED STATES OF AMERICA

DEDICATION

To all who dream wickedly and marvelously—
To all who dream!

CONTENTS

A NOTE FROM THE AUTHOR

Short stories are like decadent desserts; they're consumed too quickly, perhaps, but they stick with you for a long time after.

For readers, a good short story will surprise and delight, intrigue and startle, horrify and mystify—in short, it will provide a memorable experience. It will elicit an "Oh!" or a "Ha!" or perhaps even an emotion requiring a tissue.

For writers of short stories, the experience is similar, with the added reward of having completed a project in far less time (one would imagine) than it takes to complete something like a novel.

While creating this short story collection, I worked myself through the gamut of emotions. Inspired by odd ideas and bizarre challenges from family, friends, and an occasional contest, my stories percolated for days or sometimes weeks before insisting I write them.

Short stories are like that, you know—Pushy.

Thank you for taking a chance on this, my debut short story collection. I hope you'll find a favorite to share with a friend.

~ *Laurel*

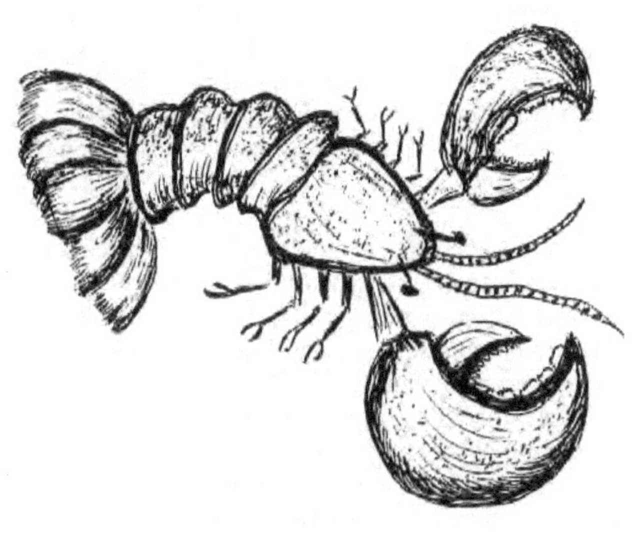

1: AS THE SHIVERING STOPS

FREEZING ISN'T THE WORST way to die. Once the shivering stops, vasodilation warms you. By then, your brain doesn't give a shit and you drift off peacefully. An intense feeling of heat could provoke you to tear off clothes, but that's not a concern.

You see, Ma Nature was cruel, gifting me with a brilliant mind encased in a paralyzed body.

And my birth mother was even more heartless. She handed me over to the scientists for a song.

For sixteen years they've used me for research, and now I've finally succeeded, though they don't know it, in opening a portal.

Best mind game I've ever solved.

I'm there now, on the other side. The creatures have taken me into their stark frigidity—countless colossal crustaceans, massive armored lobsters, crabs, and other unknown sea life with snapping claws, swirling through this bizarre multiverse, scavenging . . . and still hungry.

They study me, an anomaly in their world as in mine. Their cold presence doesn't frighten me. I've long-ago abandoned fear. And I sense they need me for more than the meat on my worthless bones.

"Let us into your world and you will walk." The leader communicates by inserting his antennae gently into my ears. "We will free you."

One blink will reopen the portal for them.

But I'll never return to that even colder world of my unfortunate birth. There will be no more probing, no more pain, no more . . . yearning. I am done.

I blink for the last time.

Abominable shrieks bounce off sterile lab walls, echoing in my brain, just as the shivering stops.

2: THE THREAT

I NEVER should have trusted her. Who was I, though, to tell Daddy that the woman who made him over-the-moon happy was someone who made me feel even deeper under it?

She moved in not long enough after Mom died.

And I can't even remember how she died—Daddy said I didn't need to know. I was five, and the only thing left in my memory now is a flash of my mother's deep blue eyes and a soundtrack I play over and over in my head.

"My beautiful baby girl."

I was her beautiful baby girl.

And then Sheila took over. Danced right into our lives and Daddy's heart. And I have to say, she was the most perfectly gorgeous woman I'd even seen. The kind you see in magazines.

"What a little cutie-pie!" She pinched my cheek the first time Daddy brought her home. It hurt, and I didn't like her, but I hadn't seen Daddy smile in such a long time. I wanted him to smile again.

I got used to having her around. Like I said, she made Daddy happy, and he never seemed to notice the little ways she kept me in my place. The flicker of a sneer on her upper lip anytime Daddy would give me a compliment. The way she'd suggest I do something with my hair, my face, my posture. Always some little thing.

"You don't want them to make fun of her," I overheard her telling Daddy one night.

"She's a perfectly normal young teen," he defended me, though I didn't know what from.

"But it's such an easy fix, and I have connections with the best in the world," she cooed. I imagined her sitting in his lap and stroking his cheek. "She could be beautiful."

"She *is* beautiful, Sheila. Always has been. All this plastic surgery makes me nervous. Little kids even asking for it now. It just isn't right."

It dawned on me that Sheila's perfect beauty may have been purchased.

"But it *is* right, Sugar Bear." I hated when she called him that. "You can't deny that rich, tall, beautiful people are more successful than the average ones. You don't want her to be at a disadvantage, now, do you?"

"Well, of course not."

I could hear the struggle in his voice. She had a point. Even I knew she was right.

"I only want what's best for our girl." She was good. She was really good.

She even got me thinking. Sure, my nose was on the big side, but it had only recently started to bother me. I always liked my eyes—they reminded me of my mother's, but I could never wear eye makeup because they were so deep. "Heavy lids." Sheila put a name to my imperfection.

And she got my father to love her. Would I ever find a good man like him to marry me with my big nose and heavy lids? He married my mom, though, and she wasn't flawless like Sheila. So maybe I'd be okay.

Over the course of the next year, she worked on me. Never when Daddy was around, though she seemed increasingly agitated anytime he'd pay attention to me. She'd buy me 'beautiful people' magazines and point out the models I could look like, if I'd only just . . .

She worked on him too, I could tell, because I'd see him looking at my nose when he'd talk to me, or around my eyes, not quite *in* them. He still told me I looked beautiful when I dressed up, and even sometimes when I didn't—that really made Sheila's lip twitch—but I sometimes wondered if his praise had just become habit.

My 16th birthday was coming up in a few months, and they called me into the kitchen one evening. Sheila looked positively giddy, but in the harsh overhead lighting, the smile on Daddy's face looked strained.

"We want to give you a very special gift for your birthday," Sheila gushed. "You tell her, Sugar Bear."

"This has to be your choice," he brushed my hair back from my cheek, "understand?"

Before he could tell me what gift I might choose, Sheila blurted, "I have a doctor who's agreed to do whatever you want, like we've been talking about!" She pulled the most recent glam mag from her bag.

"If you don't want to—"

"Of course she wants to!" Sheila cut him off again. "Look at this nose," she already had the magazine tabbed, "and this girl's eyes!" She flipped the pages before I had time to look. "And wouldn't you just die to have these lips?"

My appointment with Dr. Beauregard went well and surgery was scheduled for a month before my birthday. I'd be all healed by then, and the boys would be lining up to give me my first kiss. At least that's what Sheila promised.

She wasn't there the day the bandages came off. Some lame excuse.

And I'll never forget the look of horror on Daddy's face or the sound of his terrified shriek when the last wrap was removed.

Something broke inside him that day.

He struggles to look at me even now, but I know he still loves me, because Sheila doesn't live here anymore. How did she think this would end?

He's never spoken her name since. Pretty sure Daddy had her locked away for the deal she made with Dr. Beauregard. The authorities are still searching for him, but they'll never find him. I heard he has connections with the best in the world.

I'm sad for Daddy now because—like me—he'll probably never be able to smile again.

I cry alone in my room. I was sweet 16 and had never been kissed. Never will be kissed now, my lips a mutilated mess of flesh and the skin around my wet eyes pulled so tightly I can barely close them at night.

I was their beautiful baby girl. I remember my mother's eyes . . .

3: BERNIE AND THE BUMBLEBEES

I FOUND A FEW BODIES on the dining room table last night. I thought they were dead, but when I got close enough to see the stained glass window patterns on their forewings, they vibrated and flew into the air ducts. The heat from my face while I studied them probably revived them. I jumped back and screamed like a little girl because, well, I'll get to that.

As an acclaimed apiologist, I know there are legitimate reasons for worrying about the bumblebees. You've probably heard much to do in the news lately about bumblebee population decline in North America, Europe, and Asia—pretty much everywhere, really—and how the decline is affecting world food supply in frightful ways.

If you're fond of eating, you should pay attention now.

I've tried to warn people—I've posted statistics on all my social media sites, I've sent letters to the papers, I taped posters to light poles—but the right people aren't listening. They're not seeing what I see.

Despite our recent cultural disdain for anything without an organic, non-GMO label slapped on it, the fact is, damage has already been done to bumblebee brains by past rampant pesticide use in agricultural communities. You must know what I'm talking about. And evidence indicates their brains have been irreparably altered; the bees are forgetting where they've found their last food source.

This is not a matter to be taken lightly. If bees can't share their knowledge with their colony, they starve. They die. Crops don't get pollinated, and unpollinated crops will wither away.

Remember what I said about liking food?

And, to be blunt, we're next. We're next to wither away. We're next to die. But no one believes me.

Irresponsible overdevelopment by powerful conglomerates continues to destroy bumblebee habitats, and I'm quite certain climate change effects will not benefit the bee colonies' cause at all. This is not fake news. Regardless of the reasons, our global climate is changing, and bee populations are disappearing.

Am I making myself clear?

And I wish I could tell you those are the main legitimate reasons for worrying about the bumblebees, but there are more. Many more.

Unless you live in a cave, you've seen what I've seen these past few decades, and it's not just with the younger generations. Social media consumes more of our population's attention than any other single thing, and much like the way bee hives cannot grow when their bees are unable to do their jobs, we cannot grow as an intelligent species if we allow our brains to be placated and misinformed by corporations whose sole purpose is to keep us addicted to their products.

Addiction is bad. Certainly you must believe me.

But what does addiction have to do with the bumblebees, Bernie? you might ask. And here's where you're going to have a hard time believing me.

You see, interaction with bumblebees is directly correlated with social media addictive personality disorder. This may sound crazy, but I've studied the phenomenon extensively and committed my own monies toward purchasing the most sensitive equipment for my data collection. Although it chagrins me to know I'm the only scientist dedicated to this project, I won't sleep until everyone else wakes up.

I can tell you look confused right now, so I'll explain the phenomenon.

Bumblebees, the brain-damaged ones that remain, are far more insidious than your classic zombie when it comes to human brains. These *zombees*, for that's what they are now, don't even need to sting you to disrupt the synapses in your brain and make you want to sit for hours at a time staring at a computer or television screen. There's something in the frequency of their buzz that can eat away at the intelligent part of a human brain, which is why I screamed when they began to vibrate on the table last night.

I must not be compromised.

I can see why some in the scientific field might question my findings, and you may even have heard other explanations for why increasing numbers of humans are intellectually digressing rather than evolving. People are using excuses like, science and technology are progressing at a rate faster than we're capable of keeping up, or there's something in the drinking water, or our depleted soils aren't producing the nutrients necessary for brain development, or our schools are underfunded. My favorite excuse, of course, is from those who say, "Ignorance is bliss, isn't it?"

If you have to ask the question, you're not ready for the answer. And the answer, my friends, lies in the simple truth that the buzz of these mutant bees triggers an autonomic response whereby capillaries in the unsuspecting victim's brain shut down, halting further development and in fact, creating a rippling effect that ensures the victim will remain addicted to hype and drivel for the rest of their unproductive lives.

If that doesn't wake you up, my studies also show that once victims succumb to the buzz, they become contagious, which explains why there has been a rapid devolution in our society despite the scarcity of bumblebees in the world.

Do you see now? You don't even have to be near one of these zombees to succumb to the contagion.

And now you're probably desperate to know how you can protect yourselves from this impending threat.

I wish I had an easy solution.

My first suggestion, the easiest, is to avoid bumblebees at all cost. This should not be difficult with the current decline in their populations.

My second and last suggestion, however, will be far more difficult to swallow because you may already be infected. Although I haven't yet completed my research on how quickly this particular contagion spreads, my heartfelt belief is that if you hope to avoid the zombee contagion, you must shun ignorant individuals—you know the ones, the daytime television junkies, the gaming addicts, the online trolls—shun them as if your life depends upon it.

I also humbly request that those of you reading this will help me spread the word about this troublesome threat. Our brains are in danger. You must believe me.

Oh, no! It's dinner time. But I don't want to go back to the dining room. There will be more bodies on the table tonight, and they'll be buzzing. They'll be coming back for me. They know I'm on to them.

If it hadn't been for my startled scream when I found them last night—I startled them as much as they startled me—they would have gotten to me. And it would have been my own fault because I should have known better than to think they were dead. Zombees don't die.

"Come on, Bernie. Time for your meds. There's BINGO tonight in the dining room! Won't that be nice?"

"Poor old fool. He really believes in his zombee apocalypse theory."

"Yeah. And he used to be a university science professor."

"Just goes to show, right? Hey, can you believe what happened yesterday on *Days of Our Lives*?"

"Yeah, right? Wasn't half as exciting as Jerry Springer, though."

"Hey, check out this cat meme . . ."

4: OKAY, CUPID

I CAN'T BELIEVE it's been almost two months since the perky little ping on my cellphone told me I had a match nearby. I knew he was the kind of man I was searching for from the second I saw his photo. Something in his eyes told me Noah would more than fulfill my expectations. He looked eager, strong, confident . . . the type of guy a middle school librarian could only dream of snatching.

After I swiped right, I requested snail mail correspondence for a few weeks before agreeing to a personal meeting. I suppose I'm a bit of a romantic in that respect, and after all, I do have standards beyond the mere physical. If he couldn't string two sentences together, well, that would be an indicator of sorts. His handwriting would give me a glimpse into his personality, and the fact that he'd write any kind of letter at all would tell me if he was serious enough about getting to know more about me before meeting me in the flesh.

His first letter was sweet.

"To My Lovely Lily," it began. A good start. "Counting the days until my dreams of you become reality."

Yes, he knew how to make a new girlfriend feel desired. I hoped he didn't have a ghostwriter by his side. I've seen too many movies to know how those matches end.

Subsequent letters, which arrived almost daily, told me more about him than he probably realized. He was searching for the one to complete him, he said in nearly every letter, and just before we met, he included lines from the Billy Withers song *Just the Two of Us*:

Good things might come to those who wait
Not for those who wait too late . . .

It's funny how many songs I'd sung in the past without really thinking about the lyrics.

Anyway, the day finally came, and our first encounter was awkward—how could it *not* have been with the build-up I'd insisted upon—but I trusted my initial impressions of him.

After the first wining and dining, he was anxious to see me again, and I didn't protest. I also didn't invite him back to my house. Not yet. Not for a while, I decided. Maybe I'm old-fashioned that way, too, but if he was truly the man I suspected he was, he'd respect my wishes. For a little while, anyway.

"Oh, my God! He's so handsome!" Ruth practically drooled on my phone when I finally showed her his photo. "When were you planning to share him with us?"

I have two really close girlfriends and I'm pretty sure neither of them thought I had what it would take to lure a guy like Noah.

"This Saturday, maybe? I think he'll be okay with a little meet and greet. How about the steak house at seven?" I suggested.

"I'll tell Mary. If she has plans, she'll change them for this hunk of meat." She grabbed the phone from me an ogled him again before looking at me knowingly.

We laughed. Ruth and Mary were on a well-deserved break from the dating game. I've been lucky to have such supportive friends. You can always trust your girlfriends, you know.

The dinner date was really fun, and Noah tolerated a lot of ribbing from the trio of girls surrounding him at the table. He wrapped an arm around me frequently throughout the evening as if to let everyone know I was his—it was just what I'd expected from him in public— and I let him follow me home for the first time.

It didn't take long before Noah's behavior exceeded my expectations; I'd say it was a just a few weeks after our steak house dinner.

"I'm getting a little tired of your friends," he said, holding me so tightly that I caught my breath. "Let's stay in again tonight. Just the two of us."

Our evening rituals had become mundane quickly. Dinner and drinks and binge-watching Netflix until I coaxed him out the door, no more letters, no more attempts to make me feel special aside from his grasp around me.

Ruth and Mary had left messages of complaint after I'd cancelled on them time and time again, but I knew they'd understand. Of course they'd understand.

One night after an episode of *Stranger Things* Noah asked, "Have you put on a few pounds since we've been together?" He pinched a little flesh on my belly and chuckled. "Is that why we haven't *done it* yet? Because it doesn't really bother me, you know."

"Ouch!" I pushed his hand away, but he found other places to pinch.

He was so handsome. So fit. So . . . predictable. It was a pattern I'd seen in the movies, a pattern I'd experienced before, too.

"Maybe tomorrow night," I told him. "Come on over early, and maybe we'll skip dinner." I didn't need to wait any longer, really. I drew his mouth to mine and devoured his kiss. Damn, he was a good kisser. "Now get outta here. I'm opening in the morning."

"And maybe you'll fix up your hair before I show up. Put on a little make-up?" He pinched my cheek hard and left.

Yeah. It was a pattern I'd seen before. The only difference this time was that he was so damned handsome.

The next night, I made myself up like the prom queens in all those teen movies. I surprised myself, even. I looked pretty hot. But he didn't seem to notice. I handed him a Jack on ice with a special twist and he downed it in one gulp.

"Now we're talking," he leered at me. "Give it to me, baby!" He did a horrible Rick James impression before grabbing me roughly and biting my neck. I felt a little blood trickle down my back and flinched.

"Patience, big guy." I pushed him off of me. "I have a surprise for you, but have another, first." I poured him another stiff one and he polished it off like a pro. "I haven't shown you my special room yet." I sashayed over to a door and leaned against it as seductively as I could, like I'd seen the girls do on TV, and he pinned me against it.

I pushed him gently away from me and opened the door. "You head down first. Trust me. You won't be sorry, baby." I stole another juicy kiss before stepping aside.

He stepped through the door and started down the stairs, unsteady on his feet, as I drew the knife from my stocking.

The other two far back in the basement crawlspace hadn't been so handsome. This one almost made me feel sad, but I knew my girlfriends would understand, and they'd be happy to have me back again before our next round of dating.

It's a noble thing we're doing, weeding out the creeps, but it can wear on a girl.

I do hope to find true love someday, we all do, but until we find our perfect matches, the three of us are in this game together.

You can always trust your girlfriends, you know, and we're not stupid, Cupid.

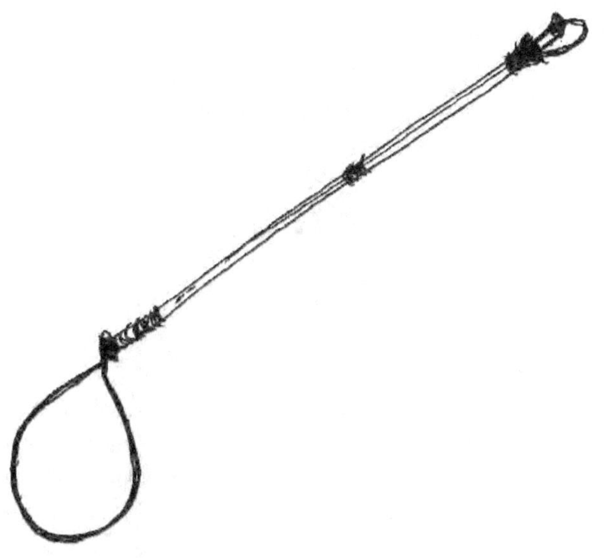

5: BAD EGGS

"LET ME OUTTA HERE, you sons of bitches! Just you wait until I get out! I'm gonna mess you up like you never bin messed up before!" The aggressive Bulldog in a crate at the end of the row wouldn't settle down.

"Don't worry, girl. I never let the bad eggs out. What's your name?"

As full-time resident of Puppy Palace Boarding Kennel, Tank made all the important decisions at night. He opened the newcomer's crate door with a flick of his Mastiff nose, and then released the other good dogs.

"Really, Tank? She don't speak no English. Check her out. Pure German Shepherd. And a real looker, too."

"I'll have you know, you pretentious little Shih Tzu, my English is quite better than yours." The German Shepherd turned her attention to Tank. "My person calls me Gretta." Stepping from her confines, she turned her tail on Sheldon, who routinely spoke and acted without thinking.

"Now, now, pretty lady, don't go gettin' all breedist on me. Didn't mean nothin' bad. Just figured you might not understand. That's all." Sheldon licked something sticky off his underside.

"What are ya, deaf? Let me outta here! You can't keep me in here forever! Whatever ya did ain't gonna last, and just you wait!" The Bulldog continued to threaten the others, but they were used to his abuse.

"Help me down, would you, dear?" Sunni, resplendent in her red EVEREADY® casing, allowed Tank to lift her from a metal wall mount. She'd been the go-to flashlight at the Kennel for as long as she could remember, and she took her job seriously. Brushing off a droplet of Tank's slobber, she sashayed over to Gretta, who appeared unperturbed by the walking, talking flashlight.

"Just don't shine your beam in her eyes. We hate it when you do that, don't we, guys?" Bruno, a goofy Boxer, stepped out of Sunni's way.

"Yes, almost as much as we hate the frequency of your flatulence," said Chauncey, an overweight Chihuahua, and they all howled. All, that is, but the lean Bulldog futilely attempting to escape his locked crate.

"All right, boys, that's enough nonsense!" Although Sunni appeared shiny and new, she sounded like an ancient spirit. Her batteries were running low. "Don't worry about that one, dear," Sunni told Gretta, indicating the Bulldog. "He'll be gone in the morning."

"I don't understand." Gretta sat demurely, attentive to the flashlight.

"She's a witch!" the Bulldog barked. "I shouldn't be here! I'm a man, I'm not a dog! Let me outta here, for the love of—"

"Silence!" Sunni aimed her beam directly into the Bulldog's eyes, and something in the tone of her voice or the glare of her light made him cower in the corner of his cage. "Allow me to enlighten you, Gretta—"

"Good one, Sunni!" Sheldon panted a hhah-hhah, but Sunni didn't miss a beat.

"—there are people out there unworthy of their companions. You're one of the luckies. I sensed it from the moment your person brought you here."

"Yes! I love my person. She cried when she left me, but she'll return with wonderful treats."

"That one, however, did not deserve the companion he brought here last week. He was, indeed, a man. A very bad man."

"Tell her about the old switcheroo, Sunni! Tell her!" Sheldon pranced in a circle, and Sunni looked at him with patient exhaustion.

"Yeah, see? I told ya so! I'm a man! Get me outta here, you sons of—"

"I said SILENCE!" Sunni continued. "Puppy Palace patrons are generally good people. It's our responsibility to ensure resident companions are healthy and safe. So when we get a 'bad egg' patron, as Tank calls them, we're bound to release the companion from their person."

Tank alerted to his name and explained further. "Sunni's pretty bright—"

"Good one, Tank!"

"—and when she senses an abused companion, she gives us a signal. Two flashes of her beam means there's a bad egg. We create a ruckus and I distract my person for just a moment. That's all it takes for Sunni to work her spell."

"The old switcheroo!" Sheldon danced on hind legs. "Person becomes companion, companion becomes person! The spell wears off the companion once they're out the door—and off they go, free to find a new person to take good care of them."

Gretta glanced sideways at the Bulldog.

"And they almost always find another person—a good person. Even stinkers like Bruno, ain't that right, buddy?"

"Yeah." Bruno farted and settled back on his bed. He had a new person now, but scars from his old person still haunted him. He instinctively avoided the Bulldog's crate, and trembled whenever a bad egg happened by.

"Aww! Don't be like that, Bruno! Come out and play! Let's teach Gretta here the ropes!" Sheldon nudged him from his bed.

"But, won't he become a bad man again?" Gretta was confused, and Tank could smell her fear.

"No," Tank explained. "Sunni makes it so the spell doesn't wear off the person. He'll stay that way till they come and get him. Come on. Let's go play in the romping room with the others."

The companions shared stories of their people and frolicked around the Palace romping room until dawn. They pretended not to hear the growls and threats and crate rattling coming from where the Bulldog remained captive in the sleeping room.

"Back to your places, everyone. They're here." Tank ensured all was in order just as a key turned in the lock.

"I don't understand it either." Tank's person spoke to a uniformed person carrying a long pole with a loop at the end. "Doesn't happen very often, but it always ends the same way. People board a nasty dog and don't come back, and I can't contact them. Funny thing is, they leave their cars here too. And look at him. No one will adopt him. Never thought dogs could be hateful, but look at those eyes. And he never stops growling."

"I'm not growling, I'm talking to you, you moron! Can't you hear me? I'm a man! That flashlight is a witch! Open this door right now!" The Bulldog raced around his crate, jumping at the bars in an attempt to escape. "And the rest of you, you just wait! You'll never get away with this! Once I'm free, I'll have you all put down!"

"This'll make him stop," said the uniform. Tank's person opened the Bulldog's crate carefully and the uniform deftly snared the frothing dog, tightening the choke around his neck.

Tank passed by the thrashing Bulldog. "Maybe you'll have it better in your next life," he told the brute before meandering outside to do his business. He watched as the uniform struggled to crate the snarling dog in the back of a truck.

When Tank returned to the Palace, he carried Sunni gently to his person, who ruffled his fur and scratched his rump.

"Time for new batteries again?" Tank's person switched Sunni off and on. "I don't know how you know these things, but thanks, buddy. You're a good boy."

Tank had mixed feelings about his role in making bad eggs disappear and would worry until the real Bulldog returned with a new person—but only for as long as it would take before the next squirrel would race across his path.

Because good boys chase squirrels, too.

6: TANKED

GULLIBLE, A DREAMER, *incurable romantic*—these accusations have haunted me for years, but I don't care. I don't see anything wrong with who I am. I'm like Popeye, except for the eating spinach part. I am what I am.

And I have the best job ever. As night shift security guard at the New England Aquarium, I get to see what most people never will. They're different at night, my aquatic friends. When all the people leave and lights in the giant ocean tank dim to moonlight, they relax.

It's not like they can close their eyes and totally sleep, but I sense a fading of fear when they see me.

They know I'm not going to bang on the barrier between us or startle them with shrieks and flashes of light. After just one year here, they trust me.

Miranda does too.

At first I thought I was dreaming. I mean, come on. What guy hasn't dreamt of getting it on with a wicked pretty mermaid? She's real, though. Night after night she returns, pressing herself against the glass between us and making me crazy.

I pinched myself hard the first time she emerged, and then screamed like a little girl when the blacknose shark appeared behind her. She laughed and showed me I had nothing to fear, latching onto the creepy creature and circling the tank with it.

Since then, we've talked about everything. I can't believe I'm the only one she'll materialize for. She made me promise never to tell anyone she's here, and why would I? She's a little bossy, though.

"Kiss me! Release me!" That's how she's been talking to me—in commands. She knows I like strong women. And I can tell she wants to be mine forever. Why else would she want me to kiss her?

But I can't let her out so easy. At least I don't think I can. How would I explain her? I guess I could say we met at work. There'd be history questions. We'd have to make stuff up. Mom might get suspicious, but all my friends would be wicked jealous. They'd never believe I could land a catch like Miranda.

And they'll want to take her away from me. So, yeah. I can't let her out without a plan.

Just last week I explained what would need to happen before our first kiss, the one that would release her from her wet world. I was getting anxious, and I'll admit it—she was starting to dominate my dreams.

"You'll need to wear clothes," I said, and then I started thinking about how I'd dress her. Tight, shimmery things, like Beyoncé wears on stage. Yeah.

"And you'll need to promise to be true to me and only me forever."

She promised.

"And you'll need to get a job cuz it's really expensive to live in Boston and my pay won't be enough for the two of us. Hey! Maybe you could get a job as a trainer here at the Aquarium!"

She thought that idea was wicked good.

"And when we have kids, they'll need to stay in *school*!" I laughed, but she didn't get the joke. There's a lot I'll need to teach her so she won't be awkward in my world. Mom always said I'd be a good teacher cuz of how I relate to little kids, so that won't be a big problem.

And now it's finally time to get her out of this tank and into my bed for real. I brought a bottle of champagne for our special moment—seemed like the thing to do—but now I wonder how it'll affect her. I don't want her staggering the first time she walks on land, so maybe I'll just let her have a tiny sip. It's expensive, so I'll drink the rest. Besides, I gotta tell you, I'm wicked nervous and excited all at the same time.

I'll drink some now before she shows up. I hope she likes her new clothes. I got them at the Goodwill, but she won't know that, and besides, the sparkly pants still have a store tag. Mom taught me how to find bargains all over town. I'm sure she'll teach Miranda too.

Boy, this champagne goes down easy. Wonder what's keeping her. I kinda feel like chuckling, but I want to be serious for our first kiss. It's important to make a good first impression. Mom always says that.

Oh! Here she is now!

I wave her over to me at the edge of the tank and she smiles one of her mysterious smiles.

"Are you excited?" I ask, and she nods, but doesn't come over to me. Instead, she waves me over to where she floats near the center of the tank. Can't believe I never thought of swimming with her.

I kick off my shoes, grab what's left in the bottle, and swim to her. Glad I'm a good swimmer.

I hand her the bottle, but she takes my face in her hands instead and kisses me in a way I've never been kissed before. I feel lightheaded, probably cuz of too much champagne. I drop the bottle and cling to her as she circles the tank one last dizzying lap.

"All right, men, let's get him outta there before the doors open. And grab that bottle too. Drinking on the job. Didn't seem like that kind of guy. Hey! Miss! You're not supposed to be in here yet!"

I watch Miranda smile over her shoulder and sashay away from a bunch of cops on the top level of the aquarium and I'm so glad she's mine. They stare at her and I'm ready to chew them out for their crude comments as they elbow one another and leer, but their boss shouts first, snapping them back to their task. They have to remove some dumb schmuck's body from the fish tank.

Hey, wait a minute . . .

Note: This story was first published on October 18, 2019 in *Whispers of the Past: WordCrafter Paranormal Anthology,* edited by Kaye Lynne Booth, available on Amazon in Kindle format.

7: TAPS

"THEM'S MY SHOES, Buford, give'm back."

"T'ain't yours, and you know my name ain't Buford."

"Okay, then, Mr. Bojangles, t'ain't yours, neither. Give'm here."

"You and whose Army gonna make me?"

I watch as Bobby and Joe fight over a pair of size 9 women's tap shoes. My tap shoes. I know I should stop them, but I'm just . . . so . . . tired. It's dark outside and the fluorescents are flickering sickly yellow and any minute now, that distant thunder's gonna be on top of us.

I feel it in the sweat covering my body, and the shivering starts.

"Gen'lemen," I whisper to the circle of residents. "Y'all are here to learn how to live in a place without roommates or curfews or metal bars."

They look at me like I've just said the funniest thing ever, and I don't know why I bother.

Especially now.

I don't know why the authorities figured that putting a halfway house at the edge of nowhere was a good idea, and I don't know why two grown men are so fixed on keeping my shoes.

I really don't know why I chose this dead-end profession, but they told me I'd be the perfect fit for this job. Momma said it was just because I was a large woman and I'd intimidate the residents. Should've listened to her.

"Would one of you please tell me where you found those shoes?"

I know where they found them. I keep them in my private bathroom at the end of the hallway, the only room in this dank place that's ever clean, because I clean it myself. If I'm on day shift, I go right to lessons from here. Night shift's the worst, but it looks like this'll be my last one.

"Danced their way right into my room last night, Missy," says Bobby, and the ensuing snickering sickens me.

"My name is Ms. Walker. You know that. You'll need to address folks by their real names, gen'lemen. It shows respect."

Bobby sticks a hand into each shoe and makes them tap on the pea-green linoleum in front of him. Joe tries to grab them, but slips on something sticky on the floor.

"Gross!" Joe scrambles back into his seat, uselessly wiping a dark stain from his pants. "That ain't right, Miss—Ms. Walker."

Thunder booms overhead, shaking the shabby building, and the lights go out. No one says a word, though several men groan. The smell of fear-sweat mixed with something metallic makes me lightheaded, and I try to ignore a tingling feeling working its way up my legs. Then, the tap-tap-tap of my shoes on the linoleum.

"Knock it off, Bobby." One of the men breaks the tense silence.

"Whaddaya mean? I ain't doin' nothin'." Bobby sounds scared.

"The shoes, Bobby," I say. I hardly recognize my own voice. "Stop the tapping."

"But I ain't doin' nothin', Ms. Walker. Don't even have the shoes no more."

I expect the emergency generator to kick on any second now, but it doesn't, and the darkness presses down on me. It's hard to breathe.

"We didn't mean for it to turn out like this, Bobby, and—"

A clap of thunder interrupts the man's uneasy objection, and a sizzling bolt of lightning illuminates several large rats, sending them scurrying away from the sticky substance on the floor. They drop my shoes when they scatter.

"Maybe we should call somebody, Bobby. You know, to fix things." Joe sounds uncharacteristically confident, and it sends a chill up my spine.

"Ain't gonna happen, men. We gotta do this ourselfs."

For a moment, I'm delighted by their decision to handle matters themselves. I've been focusing a lot on having them take responsibility for their actions lately. Maybe there's hope for them yet.

"But what'll we tell 'em?" Another anxious voice. One of the newcomers.

"We'll tell 'em she was here, we conversified about respect and how to make impressions on workin' folks, and then she got a real important call, like an emergency. We'll tell 'em we was behavin' real nice-like, and cuz of her lessons, we'd be A.O.K. by ourselfs for one night. We'll tell 'em she jus' didn't come back, and that we's worried about her."

My eyes feel heavy. I sense a shift in the atmosphere and hear several men grudgingly agree with the plan.

"Hey, I didn't sign up for this, man," the newbie protests. His chair scrapes the floor and I flinch.

"Don't matter none. Men? Make sure Boy Scout here don't tell nobody nothin'."

Bobby's in charge now and I'm . . . proud of him. I want to tell him so, but we've been trained not to single out favorites, and I'm so . . . so . . . tired.

"Bobby, please return my shoes." I'm not even sure he can hear me over the storm.

I don't know why it's important to me that my shoes go back to their clean place. The men made sure I'd never take a tap lesson again. They'll justify their actions like they always do, and their pro bono lawyers will get them off on insanity pleas.

I've done my best. Momma always told me to do my best at whatever I try. She never thought someone my size could learn how to tap dance, but I did, and I was good, too.

When the lights come back on, I look at the dripping stumps where my feet used to be. I think about the disaster the day shift will face tomorrow . . . unless these gen'lemen do the right thing for once and clean up their own mess. It could happen.

Another clap of thunder and the lights go out again. I hear a scuffle and feel a weight in my lap—my shoes! My fingers linger on the cold metal taps until I feel nothing . . . at all . . . but the cold.

8: ANCHORS AWEIGH

"IT MUST'VE BEEN hard letting him do that to your son." Steve tucked a stray curl behind my ear before nibbling on my neck.

"How was I supposed to stop him? He wanted to do it. I warned him of the potential danger, but he'd do anything for the good of the team. And sons don't listen to their moms—especially their divorced moms—when their daddy's a renowned brain surgeon.

"But, the Honor Code . . ."

"Hal has the General by the balls. It's not an issue."

~ ~ ~

My ex-husband, Hal, is a prominent brain surgeon. When the Military Academy made him an offer he couldn't refuse, he convinced me our move to West Point would be a "no brainer," an expression that quickly lost its humor, though he never tired of it.

He'd wanted to attend West Point since he was a child, but when Johns Hopkins offered him a full ride to their medical program, he made the safer decision, "the more mature decision," as his father put it, to become a surgeon. Working with cadets at The Academy was the next best thing to attending, he frequently told me, though I knew—in his mind—it would never be close enough.

Our first year there, the Army football team started winning against top-ranked teams, and after each victory, Hal would comment on how he ought to be paid more for his services. He'd never expound when I asked why, but one time he said, "Someday they'll recognize my contribution."

After a couple of years, he couldn't keep his secret any longer.

"I've discovered a way to make the players respond brilliantly to every scenario on the field," he told me after another win and a rousing celebratory romp under the sheets.

He wouldn't tell me the details, of course, but I knew it had to be some kind of brain manipulation. I started paying more attention to his pre-season activities, and noticed a slim notebook he'd hide between brain science manuals in our personal library.

If you want to hide something, do it in plain sight. I'd learned that from watching too many Bond movies. And Hal wasn't one to keep things under lock and key.

"The players are . . . too perfect," I told him after another winning season at The Academy. "You'll be found out. And then what?"

"They already know," he told me, "and it's too late now. If they start squawking, their heads will be on the chopping block too."

"But not Ray. Please don't mess with our only child's brain, Hal. He's just a boy."

"He's not a child anymore, Anne. He's going to be a soldier. He's made his decision."

I guess the stress over my constant bellyaching finally got to him.

Although the divorce wasn't contentious, I had to leave Hal and Ray, who was just starting his first year at West Point. Recruited for the Army football team, Ray believed he was invincible.

And maybe with his father's help, he would be.

Hal pretended to be horrified after our divorce when I hooked up with a Navy guy, especially the right-hand man of the Naval Academy Director of Athletics, but it was his fault for involving me so thoroughly in the historic rivalry between the two teams.

Steve began his seduction during the homecoming game our first year at West Point, and Hal was too intent on his project to notice.

"Upon the fields of friendly strife are sown the seeds that, upon other fields, on other days will bear the fruits of victory." General Douglas MacArthur spoke those word decades ago, but I know he wouldn't have approved of what Hal was doing to up the odds of victory for the Army team.

"So, Annie, you'll find out how he does it?" Steve worked his lips down my shoulder.

"It may not be easy," I said. "Sure, we're on talking terms, but that doesn't mean he'll be inviting me back into his bed anytime soon."

"Better not!" Steve tickled me and pulled me on top of him. "We might not have Mister Pretentious in our hospital, but our man's capable. The Army team's going down this year. And speaking of going down . . ."

I pushed him away, but it was another half hour before he let me out of bed.

"I need to get on the road now. Training camp starts in two days, and I'm certain that's when he does the surgeries. Think about it. The players are all isolated, they're young and impressionable—" a knot caught in my throat when I remembered my son had already gone under the knife, even though I trusted Hal's expertise unequivocally—"and they'll obey any orders they're given."

"But, how will you do it if they're isolated?"

"Let me worry about that. You've watched the movies, right? The less you know—"

He tickled me again and I slapped his hands away.

"Give me a couple of days. When I come back, you'll have what you need to even the odds this season." I dressed and threw my suitcase into the Jeep Grand Cherokee, my divorce gift to myself, and then allowed one more lingering kiss before heading out the door.

"Anchors aweigh, Annie!"

I caught myself before responding with, "Go Army, Beat Navy!" Old habits die hard. "Wish me smooth sailing!" I recovered quickly.

It was weird being back in the massive old house on Washington Street at West Point, but Hal had agreed I could stay in the guest room anytime I wanted to visit, and I missed our son terribly.

Ray hadn't forgiven me for hooking up with "the enemy," but a fleeting expression of sorrow over our broken family passed between us, and he let me hug him.

"So, you're a big sophomore now," I teased.

"We're called Yearlings, Mom." He rolled his eyes.

"Nice haircut," I said, examining his head from every angle, looking for a scar.

"You won't find one," he said. "Too conspicuous. He implants it through the nose." As if recalling a suppressed memory, Ray's nose twitched.

"Oh. That makes sense." I acted casually, as if I knew everything about the surgery. Hal evidently hadn't warned him about sharing. "Did it hurt?"

"Nah. Just a finger prick for blood and a bit of skin from the roof of my mouth. Pretty ingenious, right?"

"That's your father, all right." I wanted to know more—what did he do with those things?—but didn't want to expose my ignorance. "When will he be home?"

"Probably pretty late. He's already prepping for the newbies. Gotta run. You here long?"

"Just tonight, I'm afraid. Meeting in the city tomorrow. I'll be watching your first game, though. Can you get away for dinner?"

"I'll try. Dad keeps the fridge pretty well stocked. Just don't mess with the second freezer. He'll be using those this week."

"Roger, Roger," I said, saluting my son.

"Wow, Mom, hanging with those squids is really messing with your mind," he said, though I saw him chuckle over the *Airplane* reference as he walked out the door.

I wasted no time running to the library, but the notebook was nowhere in sight—plain or otherwise—and I checked every dust-free shelf. He must have had it with him.

To the freezer, then.

BINGO. Inside were meticulously labeled Styrofoam containers with each potential new player's name and sample collection date. There must have been twenty. I took one from the back and opened it. Inside: a microchip, a tiny vial of blood, and a sliver of skin. I removed the chip and returned the rest to where I'd found it. I'd need to find the notebook after Hal returned.

After a civil dinner—Ray brought a few of his teammates over for a quick meal before saying goodbye again—Hal retired to the library and told me to make myself at home. I can't say we'd lost our physical attraction to one another, the tension between us was delicious, but he'd made his decision, and that was that. I came up with a lame excuse for going to bed early, and waited till his footsteps passed my door later that night.

I let another hour pass, just to be safe, and tiptoed back to the library with my cellphone flashlight to find the notebook.

It was nowhere on the bookshelves, though. Thwarted again, I considered sneaking into his room, figuring he must keep it with him this close to surgery week. In my haste to leave the room—my heart was pounding in my ears—I almost missed it. Sitting smack dab in the middle of his desk in a neat stack of books and papers was the notebook.

It didn't take long to snap photos of the pages outlining the procedure, and I was back in bed with everything I needed to return to Annapolis the next morning. Time was of the essence, as they say, because the new midshipmen were starting their training too. Steve would be pleasantly surprised by my speedy return, though I couldn't take much credit for my detective work.

Hal seemed disappointed when I told him I'd be leaving after breakfast. I knew what a stressful week it would be for him, and I almost considered staying.

But no. I had important things to accomplish too.

An hour down the road, I set up at a coffee shop. I'm a pro at Photoshop, and all I had to alter was the word "cadet" whenever it preceded the word "blood" on the procedure pages. Piece of cake. I finished and took my work to the nearest printer. I was back at Steve's place by dinner.

"Monkey blood?" he asked after poring over the documents with coding for the chip and detailed procedures for how the chip, encased in a sliver of the cadet's skin and a drop of their blood, is then inserted into the brain via the nasal passage. The biomaterial would ensure secure bonding with brain tissue, and the blood, according to Hal's notes, would interact with coding in the chip, enhancing the cadet's natural abilities tenfold.

I wasn't sure how the monkey blood would interact, but I was fairly confident it wouldn't cause any undue harm to players on the Navy team.

"Yeah. Weird, right? There's a lab in the city where you can get it. I think it's the key to keeping the players pumped. You've seen how it works for the Army team."

"I guess so," he said, though he still looked perplexed. "I'll get these to our surgeon and tech team tomorrow morning. They'll be ecstatic! Great job, Annie. How's your son doing?"

"He's a man now." It was nice of Steve to ask about Ray, but I wasn't going to share anything personal about him, or how I believed he didn't need me anymore. "Oh, and he did tell me one more thing about the procedure. Seems that until there's an actual game, behavior can be a bit unpredictable. Everything kicks in at the start of the first game, though, and players become unstoppable. At least that's what he's observed."

"Should make for an exciting season, then!" He held me close and tickled my ribs.

~ ~ ~

I waited until after I knew the Naval Academy surgeon had completed his procedures before disappearing. A friend in New Zealand invited me to stay for as long as I wanted.

Navy's homecoming game was a disaster. I watched on satellite TV and laughed my ass off at the action unfolding on the field. The Navy players were all over the place, and frequently stopped in the middle of a play to beat their chests. A couple of times, players removed their helmets to pick through crewcuts with their fingers. They lost horribly, and what was even funnier was when the camera captured reactions of the coach and staff members of the athletic department. To say they appeared dumbfounded would be an understatement.

Army's homecoming was a success, of course, though one player was off his game. Must've been his sample I stole.

By the time the Army-Navy game rolled around, word had gotten out that nefarious activities had been afoot behind the scenes. Military investigators kept a low profile until after the fields of friendly strife were cleared, Army defeating Navy soundly in another hilarious show of force against their baboon-like opponents, and then it was all over.

In the hubbub of higher echelon restructuring and litigation, Honor Boards at both academies exonerated cadets of their complicity in the scam. I'll always disagree with their decision because it's common knowledge that "a cadet will not lie, cheat, steal, or tolerate those who do," and they knew they were cheating.

As for me, I think I just might find a little place here in New Zealand and stay forever. With the money the NFL deposited into an anonymous account, I don't have to worry about my future, and someday, when this scandal is forgotten, I'll reach out to my son again.

And maybe when Hal gets out of jail he'll join me. He may be pretentious, but at least he knows I hate being called Annie, and I hate being tickled even more. And, like him, I believe I've demonstrated that I'd do anything for the good of the Army team too.

Some old habits never die.

9: HUGS

HEY, BRO, BEEN MEANING to call you.

Yeah, yeah, just let me explain, okay? You know me, right? You know I'm not into all that woo-woo stuff. Never have been—

Well, yeah, except for that one time, but you did it too. I mean, come on. It's ridiculous, right? People channeling the dead? Making dishes fly off shelves? Predicting what's gonna happen to you by flipping cards? Nah. It's all bullpucky.

So . . . you're not gonna believe what happened to me on May 3rd. Remember you asked why I blew off your hockey party and I made up some lame excuse?

Yeah? Well, truth is, I wasn't ready to tell you the truth then. Sorry I missed the game, but I think what I did that night was more important. So listen.

I was on my way to your house, had the case of PBR you asked me to bring—it's still in my truck—and you know that weird little open space in the trees off 67 where we used to get drunk? Well, as I'm driving by, I notice the space is filled with this kinda flickery blue glowy color.

Of course I had to check it out! Can't believe you even had to ask. And you're the first person I'm telling this to, so just chill a minute, okay?

Okay, so I pull off in our usual spot and walk, real slow like, hiding behind the trees as I get closer.

No! I wasn't drunk yet. You know me, I don't drink and drive. And stop interrupting. This is still freakin' me out a little.

So I'm behind a tree right at the edge of the clearing and it's filled with this light like I've never seen before, and the light's filled with swirling sparkles—kinda like that glitter your sister spreads all over the place—and even though it looks icy cold, a warm, salty breeze hits my face. I can taste the salt on my lips. And you know that sound when little waves break on the beach? That's what it sounds like, real gentle and nice.

At first, I'm afraid I'll get glitter in my eyes, so I squeeze them shut, but the breeze keeps coming, and then it's like something else is nudging me forward. I wanna stay behind that last tree, but if I don't move my feet, I'll fall over, so all of a sudden I'm moving toward the light. I open my eyes cuz I have to see where I'm going, and somehow I just know the sparkles won't hurt.

Stop laughing and just listen, all right? Cuz here's where it gets real.

I'm standing in the center of the light and it's just like you see on those hokey TV shows, and, seriously, my feet leave the ground and I'm starting to lift up. It's not like how Dane Cook describes it when he talks about how the light beam sucks you up by your chest and it hurts—he's a funny bitch!—it's more like the "beam me up, Scotty," but I don't dissolve. At least I don't think I dissolved.

Hey! Shut up! I'm serious.

So the next thing I know, I'm inside this thing, or maybe I'm even outside, cuz I can't see any walls and it looks and feels like I'm in water, but I can still breathe like normal. And then—and you're not gonna believe this—these beautiful women are floating all around me.

Wait a minute, I *think* they were women . . .

It's not funny! I'm not joking around here. It was all really confusing and my head felt all messed up, but yeah, I'm pretty sure they were all women. I can't describe them, though. I can't see them in my head anymore.

How'd I *know*? Hmm. I guess it was how they felt. Their energy. It was warm and soft and . . . sparkly. It didn't really matter to me what they were, though.

So they're all floating around me and I feel dizzy and all of a sudden I hear these voices saying—no, chanting—"High five," like a chorus, all together. And I don't know what to do, so I just hold up my hand and it feels like water whooshes through it. Like, *through* it.

Don't ask me! I'm just telling you what happened.

Then they disappear, but somehow I know they're still close by. My hand feels all tingly and warm.

Gross, dude, no, I wasn't! You wanna hear the rest of the story or not?

Okay, so I'm like, "Hello? Who are you? What do you want from me?" It's not like I'm scared, because honestly, I'm feeling pretty happy, like I know everything's gonna be fine. But they don't answer, and

I'm starting to feel kinda lonely, like I know they're gonna leave too soon. So I'm trying to find them—I'm not really walking, it's more like swimming—and I see this gigantic wobbly bubble thing with a light inside that's too bright to look at without squinting my eyes almost shut.

There's something inside it, but I can't make out what it is. The aliens are floating all around it, singing that "high five" song and patting it gently, making it jiggle like Jell-O. When they see me, they whoosh over and it's like they push me back a million miles, not in a mean or scary way, but still, it takes my breath away for a minute. Guess I wasn't supposed to see what was inside the bubble.

Yeah, I know, I know, but I'm seriously telling you the truth, bro.

So then I feel like they're all examining me—

No! Not with probes, you jerk. Shut up, all right? It's like I have to pass some kind of test, and I'm dizzy again. They're all whirling around me, and kinda like when they were singing "high five," they start repeating the word "hugs" over and over again. And this part's crazy. I open my arms, and it's like they all blend together into one body to hug me.

I gotta tell you, dude, it's the best hug I can remember, and it lasts a long time. I don't wanna let go, but it starts to feel like little pieces of me are breaking away and blending in with them. It doesn't hurt, but I don't know what might happen if it continues, so I pull away, and they let me.

Why? How should I know? Maybe they just needed a hug.

Anyway, they disappear again, and I really want to follow them, but I don't. I have no idea where I am or how long I've been gone, but I don't care. I feel . . . free, like I could stay floating there forever. I'm not even lonely anymore. It's hard to describe, but it's like I've grown somehow. Like I'm more than just me.

And that's when they return.

Still wish I could describe them to you, but they're a blur in my mind. They each have a bubble with them, though, like a basketball-size version of the gigantic one they didn't want me to see, and there's something familiar in each of them. I try to focus on the one closest to me, and the thing inside stares back. And guess what.

It has my eyes.

I *am* serious! And maybe it shoulda freaked me out more, but it didn't. If felt okay. It felt like I'd finally done something right.

And then everything goes fuzzy and I hear a chorus of "goodbyes," like all their voices are combined into one but still kinda separate, and when my vision clears, I'm resting against a tree at the edge of the space and the sun's coming up. Everything's just like it usually is—no broken limbs, no crushed grass, and I feel like I've just had a really great night's sleep.

And that's what happened to me. I swear. You think I woulda missed your party for something lame?

No, I wasn't high either. You know me. I don't mess with that stuff.

Listen. I can tell you still don't believe me, so you're gonna have to check this out. I've got these marks around my back that look like glowing arms and hands, and they're still warm. Been there since they left me.

Why would I lie about this? You'll see.

No, they don't hurt—they feel good, actually, like I'm still being hugged—but how the heck am I supposed to explain them to Janice?

Oh, real helpful, dude. You're a jerk.

Go back? I don't know. I kinda feel like they got what they came for, but yeah, sure. I'll drive. Beer's already loaded. It'll be like the old days, like when we used to make fun of people like me.

And hey! Probably shouldn't share this with anyone else, okay?

Okay. Be over in ten. Yeah, just me. Bye.

How'd I do, friends?

Good? Thanks! I was a little worried he might not comply.

Yes, okay. I'll bring him to you soon.

Hugs.

1O: BABY BOOM

I SHOULDN'T BE telling you this—it's against our Code of Ethics—but if you were me, you'd have to tell someone too. It's just too astounding to keep to myself, and it's not like anyone's going to get hurt. About nine months ago my administrative assistant entered my office with an intriguing announcement.

"Ms. Knuckles? Your three-o-clock is here to see you. They say their names are Zeus and Hera. Should I call security?" She whispered that last part, and we both jumped when a lightning strike, followed by a crack of thunder, made the overhead lights flicker.

I've had some real doozies come in for marriage counseling recently, but this was a first.

"No need, Doris. I'll see them now." I was excited by the prospect of a new challenge. My clients were starting to bore me, and I was only in my second year of practice.

"What do you mean, you can't stand the way I sip my coffee?"

"The biggest problem in our marriage? It's you, you idiot!"

"What do I love most about her? When she leaves me alone for a few hours."

I've heard it all. And I'll be honest with you. I got into this line of work for the wrong reason.

"You're a lovely girl, Krindy, but let's face it. You're not exactly *Miss Personality*." My mother pushed me into an online counseling course while I was getting my bachelor's in family studies. "It'll be the perfect way to find the right man!"

I explained how unethical it would be to take advantage of what I learned from my sessions, but she maintained her position that "it's okay to break the rules once in a while."

Now, I know you'll judge me, and of course it would violate the all-sacred code, but she had a point. Not all marriages are salvageable, and I'd get the inside scoop on everything a man liked and didn't like about his soon-to-be ex. I'd be there to pick up the pieces of the one I'd choose.

Until then, I'd welcome a few eccentric new clients. Zeus and Hera, whoever they were, already aroused my interest.

From the moment they entered my office, I felt a weird vibe, and it was more than just because they were wearing cloaks. It was like I was seeing them through a hazy shimmer. I'd been meaning to cut back on caffeine, and my blurred vision was a good indicator that the time had come.

My initial impression was that they were really old, but they moved as if gliding on air. The man was strangely attractive. Powerful. Piercing eyes. And the woman was quite lovely. Maybe I was mistaken about their age.

"Mr. and Mrs. Zeus? Pleased to meet you. I'm Krindy Knuckles." I extended my hand to the woman first, but she didn't reciprocate.

"Oh, no, child. Just Zeus and Hera." She looked down her nose at me, seeming to assess me from head to toe.

"Yes. Just like Sony and Cher," the man added. "You know who we are."

His words echoed in my head, and though I didn't initially believe it, the irrational part of my brain knew it to be true.

"Krindy Knuckles. That is a name for one skilled in combat. What was your mother thinking?" Hera continued to appraise me.

"Mothers. Go figure, right? Shall we get started?" I felt it unnecessary to mention I belonged to a boxing gym.

Without hesitation, Zeus sat himself in my office chair and Hera sat on the edge of my desk, leaving me to sit on the client couch. I suppose I could have protested, but it was already turning out to be a memorable session. After reviewing the informed consent and confidentiality statements, I asked my first question. An easy one.

"How long have you two been together?"

They looked at one another and chuckled, and I suddenly felt like a third wheel.

"Far longer than you have been alive, dear." Hera had the patronizing act down to a science.

"And what made you come to counseling at this point in your marriage?" I wasn't going to let her bully me, though I already felt insecure looking up at her from the couch. Zeus's eyes bore into my own—a hint of amusement danced in them—and I felt dizzy.

"It is her idea," he said. "The woman wants a child, but asks too much of me." He sounded hurt, and I controlled a sudden impulse to hug him. Thunder rolled in the distance and I braced for the following boom.

"Let's start with that." I still couldn't pinpoint their ages—and the idea of bringing a child into an ancient marriage made me uncomfortable—but at least I had something to work with. "Hera, you want a child. Would you tell your husband why he'd be a good father?"

"Well, I am greatly fond of your strength and decisiveness and virility, darling, but that is where we run amok." She rolled her eyes like an impatient mother.

"Ah! You see? She cannot get past that essential element of my being!" Zeus's furrowed brow sharpened his rain-gray eyes and I felt drawn into them.

"Can you blame me? Never have I been unfaithful to you, husband!"

"Ah, but I have seen how you admire Thor's massive hammer!"

"Do not be ridiculous! He is but a child." Hera stood, floated behind Zeus, and placed her hands on his shoulders. "You are my husband, from time immemorial through eternity."

I had to say something, though I felt transfixed by the scene unfolding. "Hera? I sense you don't trust your husband. Should we discuss why?"

Zeus raised his eyebrows and grinned sheepishly. He was adorable. Something stirred inside me. Thunder continued to roll in the distance.

"Would you like a list of those with whom he has shared his greatest gift? Leto. Maia. Semele. Denae. Demeter. Themis. Leda—"

"Enough, sister! You have wielded your vengeance upon each, and enjoyed it."

Sister? I didn't see that coming. No wonder he'd strayed in the past, and by the sound of his floozies' names, to many foreign lands. I knew right then I had to free him from her sick clutches. He was the one for me—older than I'd imagined for myself, but strong. Decisive. Virile. It was crystal clear that Hera had been holding her holier-than-thou ax over his head for a long time. Decades, at least. I wanted him, and I could tell he wanted me too.

I had to proceed cautiously.

"Infidelity can end a marriage, I'm sure you know. And sometimes there's nothing a counselor can do." I caught Zeus's eye and did my best to convey my message. He grinned, and Hera saw it.

"Really, husband? This one?" Hera grabbed a fistful of Zeus's beard and pulled it so he was forced to look at her, and I jumped to my feet, ready to defend him.

"Release the beard!" I yelled, and immediately wondered why I'd uttered such a comical phrase. The session just kept getting better. "Step away or I'll—"

Her eyes shot me a look that knocked me back onto the couch, and then she smiled, releasing Zeus's beard and standing with her hands on her hips. "Ah! She is spirited, this one! I will approve."

"Now, dearest, let us not be hasty." He winked at me, and a wave of confusion blurred my vision again. It seemed they were messing with my mind. I had to regain control.

"I'll have you know I won't stand for violence in my office," I said with salvaged authority. "We can continue our session calmly or we can schedule another appointment. Sometimes it's helpful for me to meet one on one in order to get a better understanding of the root problems." I gave Zeus another loaded look.

"I know exactly what his *root* problem is," Hera said, and then chuckled.

I watched, surprised, as Zeus slid his hand up her robe while keeping his eyes on me. I flushed, and it took a moment before I willed myself to breathe. What was happening?

"I cast my vote for a continuation," said Zeus. "Dearest wife, please do us the favor of coordinating with the minion beyond the door and I shall join you forthwith."

It was happening. I was going to have him to myself, if only for a few precious moments. I extended my hand to Hera, but again, she dismissed me. *Foolish wife*, I thought, *leaving her lusty husband alone with a younger woman.*

The instant she left the room, I felt myself enshrouded in a cozy, warm cloud and transported back to the couch. An ecstatic shiver—like lightning surging through my veins and thunder rumbling in my nether regions—left me sprawled and panting . . . and alone.

"Zeus! Where are you? What just happened?" My breathless questions went unanswered.

He was gone.

I stood, ran my hands through my disheveled hair, and affected a casual nonchalance as I opened my office door. My heart raced.

"Doris? Did they make follow-on appointments?" It sounded like I'd just awoken. Doris scrunched her eyebrows and gave me the once-over.

"No, Ms. Knuckles. Are you . . . all right?"

I felt confused. "Did they say anything to you? Anything at all?" I tried to hide the hysteria creeping into my tone. My hands clasped my belly in an instinctive, protective gesture.

"They barely acknowledged me," she said, "but they were holding hands and giggling as they left, so congratulations!"

"Congratulations? What do you mean?"

"On helping them overcome their issues, of course. You've helped them rekindle their love!"

I ran back into my office to throw up in the trash can, and that's when I noticed it. Zeus had left his cloak on my office chair—a clear indication that he'd be coming back to me.

But that was nine months ago. The only thing that kept me motivated as my belly grew was my certainty that as soon as our child was born, Zeus would return to claim us. I could see it in his eyes, and I could feel it— oh, boy, could I feel it!—when he disappeared on me that tumultuous day.

So when I awoke this morning to cold, wet sheets, I knew what had happened wasn't just a dream. Zeus and Hera *were* by my bedside last night, and the beautiful baby boy I'd been nurturing—the baby who was in my womb one moment and in Hera's arms the next—would never be mine.

"What will you call him?" Zeus's whisper echoed in what I thought was a dream.

"How about Knuckles? Just look at the size of his fists!"

I saw them smile, and knew my baby would be safe.

"And you will not strike vengeance upon she who has been our vessel." Zeus's decree was unnecessary, though I was grateful for it.

Now you know why I had to tell you my story. I broke the rules, yes, but they played me, and played me good. I was wrong, though, about no one getting hurt. From the looks of me, you'd never know I'd carried a baby to term. That's a godsend, but how am I to recover from my shattered expectations?

At least Zeus left me his cloak. I wrapped it around myself before changing my sheets, and noticed something sticking out of a pocket. I pulled out a sheet of paper on which lightning-bolt-shaped letters read: *Krindle Knuckles is a Knockout!*

I smiled, canceled my appointments for the rest of the week, and registered for an upcoming boxing tournament. I think I've finally heard my calling.

"Take good care of him!" I shouted at the ceiling.

Thunder rumbled, a single lightning strike flickered my bedroom lamp like a wink from Zeus, and gentle rain danced on my rooftop.

11: SCORING LOVE

"TELL ME YOU'RE NOT going to entertain such lunacy, Blain!"

"Lunacy? Oh, my darling! You hurt me to my very core! Have you no faith in me? In my abilities?"

"But you mustn't! You simply mustn't! What will happen to me if you—"

"Oh, but I must! I do this for you, my little sugar plum! When I win this match, you'll see. You'll see how they'll look at me, how they'll invite me—us—to all the posh events. You want this as badly as I, my darling, I just know it!"

"But your neck—the brace—"

"A minor hindrance, my sweetness. It will offer a fairer fight for my lowly opponent—Giles never could return any of my serves—and the crowd will be on my side. Surprised he actually signed up for this match knowing he'd have to play me. I'll make short work of it. Now, don't you worry your pretty little head about anything."

"But I *do* worry, Blain! The surgeon said—"

"Phooey on the surgeon! Pompous ass, telling me I'd be out of commission for months. Look at me, my darling! Does this look out of commission to you?"

"Well—"

"No, of course not. Now, help me with my bags, would you, honey-bear?"

"But he said that if you re-injure—"

"What he said is pure malarkey, my little love muffin. Now, the bags. And have you bleached my Sunday shorts?"

"Of course, Blain. I always bleach your outfits. Why would you ques—"

"Oh, *ma chérie*, forgive me for my impertinence! You know how I get before these events. Come! Come into my arms and tell me how much you love me."

"I lo—"

"There, there now. All better. Time to get a move on. You wouldn't want me to miss my first set, would you?"

"Well . . ."

"I'll be rooting for you, Blain, and I—"

"I know you will, baby. Just don't distract me with that beautiful face of yours, okay, sugar?"

"No, of course not, but please be—"

"A winner? Don't worry, sweet pea, I've got this!"

"Blain! I was going to say, I want you to—"

"I know, I know what you're going to say, and I want *you* to know I love you too, my darling. Now, off I go!"

"Hello, Giles, let's give the cameras what they're looking for, shall we? Show them what great *pals* we are?"

"Bone-crushing handshake as always, Blain, but you really shouldn't be here right now. I mean, come on, man! A tennis match in a neck brace? You're that desperate to prove yourself? Poor Clementine. She must be worried sick."

"Enough small talk, Giles, and leave my woman out of this. I won her years ago, and the coin toss just now, so you're the one who should be worried. I serve first."

"All right then. May the best man win."

"Out!"

"Out!"

"Out, out, damned umpire! When was the last time you had your eyes checked? Okay, okay! *Sorry.*"

"Love-fifteen."

"Love-thirty."

"Love-forty."

"Game."

"Dammit!"

"Come on, Blain. My serve. And let's remember a little court etiquette, *shall we*? Or maybe you should withdraw now, really. There's no way you can win this. And honestly, I don't want to hurt you. It's bad enough I'm playing against a—"

"A what? Say it!"

"An asshole. There. You happy? I'm playing against an impaired asshole. Now, give me those balls."

"Fifteen-love."

"Thirty-love."

"Forty-love."

"Game."

"Dammit to hell!"

"Let's go home, Blain. Thank God you didn't get hurt again."

"Didn't get hurt? I lost the match to Giles, my pet! To *Giles*! How can you say I didn't get hurt?"

"You know what I mean."

"Of course I know what you mean. But you don't understand what this loss means for me. This loss—"

"You risked crippling yourself over a stupid game, Blain. And where would that have left me?"

"It would have left you where you've always been, *mon chou*, right by my side."

"Yes, right by your *bed*side as your nurse and maid. You're destined to enslave me again through your irresponsible behavior, aren't you?"

"Oh, my darling, hush, now. Giles is coming over, and the cameras. Please behave, and turn that frown upside down."

"Well played, Blain, especially under the circumstances. And Clementine? You're looking well. Blain's a lucky man."

"If I were lucky, old chap, I'd be attending tonight's award dinner, not you."

"Don't listen to him, Clementine. I'd say the luckier man gets to go home with you tonight."

"Careful, friend. Don't even try to score points with my woman. She loves me. Don't you, sweetie?"

"Love? Love? There are no *points* in love, Blain. And you know what? I'm not your little sugar plum. I'm not your honey-bear, and I'm certainly not your pet."

"But, darling—"

"No more *darlings*! No more *sweet peas*! Do you even remember my real name?"

"Of course I do, love bug! And you're right. It's time to go home for some R and R before my next match."

"No. I won't be going home with you tonight, Blain, and you know what? I'm finished playing your little love game. It's always been just a game for you, hasn't it? And I've always been your little trophy, haven't I? NO! Don't open your mouth! You're not going to cut me off again! I've had it with your patronizing idiocy! This is a game I never win, and no! Don't you dare say another word! Just zip it! All this talk of love—well you can go home and love yourself, for all I care right now!"

"Ouch, Blain. Serves you right, *old chap*."

"Let's get out of here, Giles. I deserve better than this."

"No! Don't leave me. Don't do it. Oh, my darling. No, my darling Clementine. Clementine? Clementine!"

12: BILLY'S GIFT

"HEY! BILLY! What the hell's wrong with you? Can't you hear? Answer the goddamn phone, you worthless twerp." Billy's father mumbled the last several words, but Billy heard them. He always heard them.

Billy missed his mom. And he hated his father. He blamed the belligerent, burly man for his mother's death five years earlier, though the investigators never found any proof. And who would have believed a four-year-old child as an eyewitness?

Losing her when he was four was confusing and terrifying, but having to live with the man who took her away from him, the man Billy had mutely pointed his finger at when the police finally arrived that horrible day, was a struggle that had grown more intense each year. After the hubbub surrounding her death had passed, Billy had to explain to his pre-school teacher how he had broken his pointer finger "by getting it stuck in the swing set."

He had no swing set.

The strident sound of the telephone made Billy's ears hurt. Like his father's voice, it was always too loud.

"Billy?"

Like now.

Over the years, Billy learned from experience that his father knew where and how to hurt a person. But how could his teachers and the police have missed all the other signs of secret abuse? Sure, some of the officers were his father's friends from high school, but when they were in uniform, weren't they supposed to arrest bad guys?

Billy's father was a bad guy.

"NOW, goddamn it! You don't want me gettin' outta this chair—"

"I g-got it!" Billy ran to the mustard-colored telephone mounted on the grimy kitchen wall and grabbed the receiver. "Hello, M-m-Monroe residence, B-Billy speaking." He glanced into the room where his father sat in his recliner watching a college ballgame. The stack of empty Bud cans on the floor by his right hand looked like a crumbled cartoon tower. Billy would have to collect them soon, but not while his father was drinking.

"Listen carefully, Billy," a woman's soft voice spoke. "Tomorrow while your father is at work, a package will be delivered to your house. It is a gift for you, but you must not show your father. Hide it somewhere he will not find it. Now, hang up and tell him this was a wrong number."

The line went dead. Billy stared at the receiver for several seconds before hanging up, baffled by a tickle of delight in his stomach. He was going to get a present in the mail. A surprise present, just for him. His father had forgotten his 7th, 8th, and 9th birthdays, and Christmas was just another day since his mother's death.

A gift. Just for him.

"Wrong n-number," he told his father, who grumbled. Billy cleaned the dishes piled in the chipped porcelain sink, brushed his teeth, and hurried to his bedroom, where he'd stay till his father would holler at him the next morning.

His tiny bedroom was immaculate. It wasn't difficult to keep it orderly, as Billy didn't have much. A jacket, two pairs of jeans and three shirts hung evenly spaced on plastic hangers in the doorless closet. His frayed sneakers and one pair of "good" shoes, too tight for him now, looked lonely on the floor beneath the hangers. A blue plastic bin held his socks and underwear. His walls were bare, save for one poster tacked next to his bed—a freebie given to all students after a health fair. "Milk! It Does A Body Good," it read. At least it was colorful, and the man with the milk mustache looked happy.

It took Billy a long time to fall asleep. He was used to the blare of the television in the next room, but he was not used to the feeling of excitement rumbling in his stomach and making his mouth turn up at the edges. He couldn't wait until tomorrow.

"Get up," his father's voice boomed, "and clean up the mess in the living room before you leave." His bedroom door slammed against the wall when it swung open. "I won't be home till late. You better do good in school. There's a couple'a hot dogs left for dinner." The man lumbered out of the house and drove away.

Billy stretched, used the bathroom, and shuffled to the kitchen. There was one frozen waffle in the freezer, which he popped into the toaster. The drizzle on the kitchen window told him it would be a day like most others in Portland, but then he remembered the phone call.

It was probably a wrong number. Was probably just a prank call. He shook his head and kicked the cabinet. "S-stupid," he sputtered, and after washing down the dry waffle with what was left of the milk, Billy dressed and walked to school, his feet cold from the steady rain seeping through his sneakers.

Although he never felt horribly out of place among his peers—many of their fathers worked in the forest industry like his father—he didn't have a best friend. All the other kids had mothers. And none of them stuttered.

Mostly, Billy felt invisible.

All he knew about his father's work was that he cut down and chipped up trees for a living. He drank a lot and cussed a lot and stayed out late a lot. Billy was okay with him staying out, and was a pro at being in bed, pretending to be asleep, when his father returned on those late nights.

Since his mother's death, Billy was convinced nothing good could ever happen to him. Still, he ran home after school. Maybe. Just maybe. He paced around the small house for about an hour, tidying up his father's mess and peeking out the front window every time he passed it. Finally, with nothing left to clean, he turned on the television and sat in the only chair in the room.

Excitement and disappointment overwhelmed his body and brain, and he fell asleep in the recliner.

Billy jumped when the doorbell rang. Groggy from his unexpected nap, he stumbled to the window and peered through a slit in the drab draperies. A man in a uniform waited at the door holding a box, but Billy knew not to open the door to strangers when he was alone. He hid beneath the window, his heart racing, and prayed the delivery man would just leave the box and go away.

Another clamorous clang of the doorbell set Billy's nerves on edge, and he squeezed his eyes closed. He hoped the man outside wouldn't hear his heart beating, wouldn't smell his fear.

Finally, he heard a door slam and a truck pull away. He peeked out the window and saw the man was gone. The box remained on the front step. It wasn't very big. It didn't have any colorful ribbons around it. It didn't really look like gifts he remembered from when his mother was still alive, gifts he'd seen in commercials, gifts he'd seen other people get—but there it was.

And it was only five o'clock. His father wouldn't be home till late, and that meant nine or even later. Billy opened the door and stared at the box for a moment before lifting it as if it were a baby bunny. It weighed almost nothing, and when he shook it gently, ever so gently, he heard a metallic jangle.

He hurried the box to his bedroom and shut the door. Sitting on the floor with the box between his legs, he read the label. "For Billy," was all it said. No postage, no return address, just, "For Billy." He didn't know if the goosebumps on his arms were from fear or excitement, but it didn't matter. He opened the box.

When he pulled out the little brass lamp, he laughed, startling himself by a sound he hadn't made in years. He knew the story of Aladdin and had watched some dumb old "I Dream of Jeannie" shows after school, but who would send him a brass lamp? The gift was silly.

It didn't matter, though. It was a gift, and it was only for him.

He looked around his room for a place to hide it, and while there weren't many good places, he knew his father would never look in his underwear bin. Walking over to his closet, he absentmindedly ran his hand over the cool, smooth brass surface.

And it vibrated.

He dropped it in fear and watched as mist poured from its spout.

"N-n-no, w-w-way!" His eyes opened wide as the vapor condensed into the form of a plump little old woman, too round to look good in a harem outfit, but wearing one nonetheless.

"Hello, Billy." Her voice was sweet—she sounded like the prank caller—but this couldn't be a prank. Billy stepped toward her and hesitantly touched her fleshy arm to make sure she was real. "I am real, young man, and I am here to grant you three wishes."

"B-b-but how c-can this b-be real?"

"You must believe I'm real for your wishes to come true. Is there anything you wish for, Billy?"

"Y-yes! Of c-c-course! I w-w-wish I d-didn't st-st-stutter anym-m-more!"

"Your wish is my command, then, if you believe."

"I do! I do! I DO! Hey! It worked! You did it! It's gone! My stutter is gone!" Billy jumped up and down and spun around, laughing, until he fell to the floor. "How'd you do it? Who are you? Who sent you to me? What's your name?"

"I am called Adea the Kind, and you have two wishes remaining. Use them wisely, Billy. You do not have to choose your wishes all at once. Perhaps you might wait before sharing your next wish with me. I hear your father approaching. Do not let him find me."

"Then . . . go back into your lamp! Hurry! I'll hide you!"

Adea returned through the spout and Billy stashed the lamp beneath a heap of yellowed socks in his underwear bin. He felt embarrassed, and hoped the genie wouldn't know where she was. He wondered why his father had come home early.

The man was in a foul mood. "You better'a lef' me one of them dogs, Billy!" He opened the refrigerator door and slammed it shut. Billy heard the microwave going and waited for the high-pitched beep to stop before joining his father.

"I thought you'd be out late," said Billy.

"Whad'you say?" The man pulled Billy toward him by his collar, twisting it in a way that made him choke a little.

"I-I-I thought y-you were g-going to b-b-be late. Th-that's all." It felt strange to have to force a stutter, but Billy couldn't let on that he'd been cured.

His father reeked of alcohol.

"Whass it to you, you little tard? You mind jor own binizz." He smacked Billy on the back of the head hard, sending the boy into the kitchen wall.

When he stopped seeing stars, Billy glared at his father and ran to his room.

"Run away, lil baby, run away," his father's slur trailed off.

The next morning, his father left for work without saying anything to Billy, and Billy knew what his next wish would be. He released Adea from her brass confinement before leaving for school.

"I wish my father would never, ever, ever hit me again." Billy's chin quivered.

"Remember, Billy, you must believe I am real for your wishes to come true. Do you believe? And is this truly what you wish?"

"Yes. I don't want him to ever touch me again." He rubbed the bump on his head.

"Your wish is my command," she said. "Now, hide me and go to school. You have only one wish remaining, Billy. Consider it wisely." She turned to mist and returned to her lamp.

Billy returned his gift gently to the safe place in his bin. For the first time since he could remember, he felt happy. Adea had taken away his stutter, and now she would make sure his father wouldn't hit him again. He wondered how her magic worked. He was excited to talk to his classmates. Maybe he'd have a chance to make real friends now that he didn't stutter anymore.

Shortly after getting to school, however, he was called to the office.

"Hi, Billy." The school counselor met him and brought him into the Principal's office. "I'm afraid we have some bad news about your father." Billy braced for the news. "It seems he's had an accident at work. He's in the hospital now, but I need you to be prepared when you see him."

For a moment, Billy expected to hear that his father was dead. It surprised him that the thought did not make him sad. He waited for the bad news. "It was one of the machines," the counselor continued, "it trapped his arms inside. He'll probably never be able to use his hands again." She looked at Billy intently.

It took a moment for the words to make sense. *Never be able to use his hands again.* Billy's eyes grew wide when he remembered his second wish, and he felt goosebumps rising on his arms again. He couldn't quite identify a new feeling in his stomach.

"We'll take you to see him when the surgeons say we can. Is that okay with you, Billy? And is there a friend you can go home with after school?"

"Yes, ma'am," Billy lied.

"I think you should stay in school today," she said. "There's nothing you can do, and it will keep your mind from worrying too much. He's in good han—I mean, the doctors will take good care of him. Okay?"

"Yes, ma'am," he repeated.

After school, he ran home and summoned Adea. "Thank you, Adea. My father will never hit me again." He wanted to feel happy about the news, but his stomach felt unsettled when he tried to imagine his father without hands. It was a little scary.

Adea looked at the boy, her brow furrowed, her eyes filled with compassion. "Oh, but the sorrows you have endured, child . . ."

Billy looked into the old woman's eyes and his chin quivered. Tears washed his soft cheeks and he trembled. "I miss my mom. I want my mom. Please bring her back to me. I know what I want for my last wish—I want you to bring my mom back to me." He sobbed, and waited, but Adea didn't move. "Please! I want my mom! I have one more wish. I've thought about it a lot, really. You have to bring her back! Bring mom back to me!"

"Oh! My dear, dear boy. Even with your strongest belief, this is one wish I cannot grant. Never has a genie been allowed to bring back one who has passed to another realm. I am sorry."

"But it's not fair! When my father comes home, he'll find another way to hurt me! And I'll never have any friends now. It won't matter if I can talk like them. I don't have a mom and my father's going to be an angry, horrible monster! What do I have left to wish for if I can't get my mom back?"

Adea waited until Billy stopped ranting.

"I cannot bring your mother back, Billy. But there is one thing I can do."

"What is it? Tell me!"

"I can . . . bring you to her." She spoke the words softly.

Billy took a moment to consider what that might mean. It could mean something scarier than his father's accident. But he didn't see how it could be any scarier than what his life would be like once the mangled man returned from the hospital.

"Yes. Yes! Bring me to her! I don't care what you have to do, what *I* have to do, please bring me to her now! I believe in you, Adea, and for my last wish, I wish for you to bring me to my mom!"

"Your wish is my command, then, Billy. Now, come to me."

Adea opened her arms to the boy, who stood for a moment before moving. He wiped his eyes and face with his sleeve.

"Wait a minute," he said, tucking in his shirt. He removed his threadbare sneakers, placed them neatly in his closet, and squeezed his feet into his good shoes. He combed his fingers through his hair, and then rubbed the goosebumps from his arms.

"How do I look?" he asked the genie.

"You look like a fine young man. Now, come to me. She is waiting."

Billy stood tall, stepped toward the woman, and allowed himself to be enveloped in her soft, warm, full arms, arms that seemed to expand as they wrapped around him, hugging him in a steadily constricting embrace that was so soft . . . so warm . . . so quiet . . . so safe . . . so . . .

13: ORBS

LOLLY THOUGHT she might be insane.

She'd communicated with her orb since before she could speak her first word, but when she turned five, it told her she needed to pretend it wasn't there. She wasn't to point to it or speak aloud to it or talk about it anymore, and she wasn't to acknowledge other people's orbs either.

They will never understand. They will make fun of you, it had told her. *We can hear the voice inside your head, and you can hear ours. This is how we will talk from now on.*

She was sad. She liked chatting with her orb.

Lolly's parents seemed relieved when she stopped *playing with her imaginary friend,* as they liked to call her bizarre behavior. They had tried everything to get their little girl to act like other children. They were especially unsettled by the way her eyes always focused on a point somewhere above the people interacting with her, never in their eyes. And she'd say things about other people. Things she shouldn't know.

"She's so precocious," the older ones would say, and then they'd avoid her.

Doctors found nothing unusual about her physical development, nothing concerning about her vision, and suggested more play time with children her age.

Decades passed, and Lolly learned how to look into people's eyes when she spoke with them. She was sixty now, and pretty sure she was insane.

If she weren't a brilliant journalist, others might agree with her, but her reputation as an international reporter had earned her adulation and awards over the decades. She insisted on traveling alone and taking her own photos and videos. No one could get to the bottom of a story like Lolly could. Time and time again, she'd discover an unlikely source, breathe life into a dead lead, and unearth the missing piece of a puzzling story.

No one knew how she did it.

And she could never tell them how. They'd never understand, and at her age, they'd do more than make fun of her.

It is time to find them, her orb told her when she awoke on the first day of her sixth decade. *Three fertile couples on each of the seven continents except for Australia, where you will find two. The third you will find in New Zealand. They have not yet found their mates. You must bring them together.*

"But, how will I find them? Can't you just tell them what to do, where to go?" Lolly spoke aloud when she was home alone, which was always, when she wasn't working. She'd suppressed her communication far too long in her youth and decided early on never to bring a partner into her unusual reality.

They have not accepted us as you have. None on your planet has—none but you. You will know them by their orbs. Couples who are to be together will have orbs that glow the same hue.

"They'll think I'm crazy! They'll—"

They will be joyful. You will liberate them from their secret. They will believe you because you understand.

"Six people on each continent—"

Except for Australia—

"Yeah, yeah, I get it. You want New Zealand to be a continent, but still—how the heck—"

There will be stories for you on each continent. You will be sent to cover them. We will guide you to the individuals. They won't be far from each story.

"All right, then. What's my first lead?"

The disappearing continent. Antarctica. You will bring together environmental scientists from different nations working on similar essential projects. You will be tasked . . . now.

Lolly's phone rang just as her orb finished speaking.

"On the red-eye tonight? Got it. First class? Wonderful! Thanks, boss!" Lolly hung up and repacked her "to go" bag for a climate harsher than she was used to.

"And what am I supposed to say when I find these people? 'Hey, I see my orb too, and boy do I have a proposition for you'? Something like that?"

Something like that, yes. They will know when they see you. We will talk to them. When they see you, they will finally be ready to listen.

"You know I don't speak all the languages, right?"

We know. It will not be necessary. You will be understood.

"Okay, so what's going to happen after I finish playing matchmaker on all these continents?" She braced for the answer.

There was an uncomfortably long pause before Lolly's orb spoke.

You know what will happen.

Lolly knew what would happen, but she didn't know how it would happen. And she didn't necessarily want to believe it.

And she still considered the possibility of insanity.

Her first assignment was to report on the frightening meltwater lakes threatening the ice shelves surrounding Antarctica, a topic about which she knew little. Arriving rested from her first-class accommodations, Lolly was escorted to several University research teams over the course of her three day project.

Her preeminence in the media was helpful.

Finding her three couples was easy. Getting them together was not as easy as her orb had promised. Despite her reputation, Lolly had a hard time convincing the scientists to speak with her privately—a necessity for the real work she was doing on the continent.

Only two of the six had eyes that flashed when Lolly introduced herself. They knew right away they were chosen for something far greater than their research. The other four feigned incredulity when they finally consented to speak with her.

Their typical response surprised her: "I know what you're saying, and theoretically speaking, I see your orb—and mine, but I'm a scientist, for goodness sake. We mustn't speak of it. This doesn't fit our world."

She thought they'd be more open to exploring their anomalies.

"Just . . . find a way to be with this person when your orb tells you it's time," Lolly told them. "Trust me. Much like your work here, it's of global importance."

That got their attention.

Lolly delivered her sensational story just in time to receive her new lead about a dramatic shift in gun legislation on the tiniest continent. She found her couple within moments of stepping into a rowdy crowd chanting around the New Zealand Parliament Buildings. The man and woman were in different crowd clusters, and the noise and heightened excitement allowed her to slip up to each of them unobtrusively.

She whispered into the man's ear first. He dropped his sign and stared at her, wide-eyed, before looking up at her orb. He walked with her to the outskirts of the gathering and over to where they could see the glow from the woman's orb.

"I'll speak to her first," Lolly told him, and disappeared back into the crowd. She smiled at the expression of anticipation on the man's face.

Moments later, she reemerged with the young woman behind her. The man smiled meekly, and the woman didn't hesitate in extending her hand to introduce herself to him. They were anxious for answers, but Lolly was not to tell them any more than she had. They were to be a couple. That was all.

Australia was a fluff piece compared to anything she'd previously reported on—the discovery of a deadly new species, a troubling cross between a snake and a spider.

One couple with matching orbs worked as educators in different cities, and the other young man and woman had just graduated from their respective high schools.

"No way! Seriously?" The young woman did a little happy dance when Lolly said, "Yes way!"

Finding and matching couples on the continents of Asia, Europe, Africa, and South America presented unique challenges as Lolly continued to crank out in-depth features on scandals and corruption and unpopular legislation. Her orb told her everything she needed to know, so at least the stories weren't difficult to write.

When Lolly returned to the North American continent for her last stories, she felt sad. None of the people she knew had matching orbs.

"But, I know this amazing couple in my town! They're already together, and—"

No, Lolly. Find the ones we have chosen.

Her head felt fuzzy for a few moments.

Three more months passed while she completed stories on civil unrest and viral epidemics and an upsurge in UFO sightings, successfully matching three more couples in the process.

She finally returned, exhausted, to the relative quiet of her apartment. She considered adopting a cat.

You have done well, her orb whispered as she fell asleep. It had been nearly two years since it had sent her to Antarctica. *Consider what may come, and prepare.*

Weeks passed, allowing Lolly time to consider her life and her options. Bone-weary, she nevertheless forced herself to connect with friends long put on hold till she'd have time for them. Some of her visits were joyful; others, exhausting litanies of loss and illness and wishes unfulfilled.

It is time, her orb told her as the sun rose on the vernal equinox. *But the decision is still yours.*

Lolly's joints ached after a restless night of fitful dreams. She gave her orb a sideways glance and flipped on the news.

Bombings. Riots. Lies.

Outside, rush hour traffic already clogged her street. Buds struggled to open on the fragile maple surrounded by concrete outside her window. She thought of the unlikely couples and wondered how their relationships were progressing.

She wondered how they'd handle life in a brand new world, twenty-one couples alone on a planet wiped clean when the orbs would deliver their final message to their people.

And she would not be spared.

Yes or no, Lolly. Yes? Or no?

I still might be insane, she thought, *and if I am, then—*

The television hissed static.

Note: This story was first published on October 18, 2019 in ***Whispers of the Past: WordCrafter Paranormal Anthology***, edited by Kaye Lynne Booth, available on Amazon in Kindle format.

14: FINE PRINT

"IT'S A REALLY QUIET neighborhood, babe, you're gonna love it!"

For the past few years, Perry and I have been searching for the perfect place to raise our children. City life is killing us, and Perry's new job allows us to settle down, finally, in one of the lovely neighborhoods in a little town called Leadville. We've vacationed there frequently, and the idea of living in an old, Wild West mining town has always frightened and fascinated me—frightened, because I grew up accustomed to the comforts of an east coast suburb, and fascinated, because I've always loved a good challenge.

Why not give this very different lifestyle a try?

Perry is super focused on moving us soon, too. He met with a realtor last week while I was working. I'm pretty excited, and the kids think it'll be like a TV adventure.

"We'll have several choices. I think you and the kids will be happy with any of them."

"And it's walking distance to school?" I ask.

"You can see the elementary school from all of them," he tells me.

I try to imagine what it'll be like not to have to worry about bus schedules and traffic jams.

We're at the realtor's office ready to tour our potential new neighborhood, and Perry's right; there are several homes available, and the prices are nothing compared to what we've been paying in the city. I introduce myself to Mary.

"How long have you been selling homes here?" I ask.

"Oh, 'since Hector was a pup,' as my father used to say. Can't remember a time when I wasn't in real estate!"

Mary charms the children with her bouncy attitude and bowl of treats.

"Is this Trick'r Treat?" Raphael, our 7-year-old, is all about the treats, and it just so happens to be October 31st. Perry and I plan to surprise the children with new costumes and a stroll around town later this evening.

"Tricky treat!" Almost four, Angela does her best to mimic her brother. I'm happy they're so close; Raphie will be a wonderful big brother when Angie's old enough to worry me.

"We'll talk about Trick or Treat after we look at some cool houses, okay, kiddos?" Perry ruffles Angie's golden ringlets.

"There's plenty of room in my car if you'd like me to drive! That way, I'll be able to answer any questions you might have!"

We load into Mary's Subaru Outback and I notice its pristine interior. It smells of astringent and something familiar, though I can't quite identify it. I pull back Angie's hand when she reaches out to draw designs on the condensation inside my window, and I give Raphie a look that tells him to keep his hands to himself, too. It's a message I've relayed more than a few times in his more than a few years of life.

I wonder about how we'll all adapt to the cold. It's already snowed here, and the pumpkins are covered in frost. *We can do this*, I tell myself. After all, just think of what the early settlers endured. No Gore-Tex, no insta-meals, no running water . . . yeah. We'll survive.

"So much stone!" I share my observation about many of the yards we pass.

"Xeriscaping is popular here, especially since the growing season if so short." Mary looks at me in her rearview mirror. Her eyes look blurry in the mirror. Must be the condensation, or the extra-heavy makeup someone seems to have caked on her face. There's no way she would have applied that much herself. An overly-zealous daughter, perhaps?

"And I guess Halloween's really popular, too. There must be a sale on plastic headstones at True Value!" I say. Too many headstones for my taste, but hey, we're in the Wild West now, and it *is* Halloween.

Mary smiles and fidgets in her seat.

"Can I get one? And Angie, too?" Raphie asks, and I tell him we'll see if there are any left later on. They've certainly come a long way with lawn decorations. Several of these look authentic.

"Here's the street with the homes Perry toured last week. We'll start here." Mary pulls into a fairly nice driveway and I see an old man sitting on his porch a couple of houses down. A floppy hat covers most of his pale face, and I wonder if he's ill.

"There's gold in them there hills!" he shouts, pointing toward the Mosquito Range.

I chuckle and wave at him, but he doesn't wave back. Some of the Aspens in the hills still cling to their golden leaves, but for the most part, autumn colors have faded. As Robert Frost aptly acknowledged long ago, "Nothing gold can stay."

"He's a funny old soul," says Mary. "Lots of wizened veteran miners in town. They're standoffish, but it does make for a peaceful neighborhood."

From the front yard, the elementary school is a stone's throw away.

Despite a chilly interior, the first house is more than adequate for our needs, and there's a decent yard. Plenty of space to put up Halloween headstones and other holiday decorations.

All three homes are perfect, though I wish the realtor had turned on heat before we toured them, and we unanimously agree we'd like to live in the one on a corner lot.

"All that's left to do is the paperwork!" Mary is positively buoyant over our decision, and for a moment, she seems to lift from the ground. I really need to get more sleep, but excitement over this move has kept me awake nights, and people say Leadville's elevation can make you feel weird.

Back in Mary's car, I finally put my finger on the subtle secondary odor—formaldehyde—and I'm transported back to my high school biology class the day the dead earthworms are delivered. Yuck. As much as I want to ask Mary about it, I decide I really don't need to know about her extracurricular activities.

We make quick work of signing the sizeable stack of documents, laughing about how long it would take if we actually took the time to read through every page, and when we get to the last document, Mary calls the children over to the table.

"What do you think? Would you like to sign, too?" She smiles at us and winks, and Raphie's the first to grab a pen.

"Look! I can write my name real good!"

We laugh. I've helped him practice cursive writing this year, and he signs his name in all of his new books.

"Me too! Me too!" Angie grabs the pen and adds her scribble, and the two disappear to a toy-filled corner in the office.

"Well, I suppose that's it!" Mary looks at us expectantly, and then . . .

"I feel funny, Perry," I whisper.

"You *are* funny, babe! It's one of the reasons I love you so much!"

"No! I mean, I don't feel right. I feel—"

"It's just the altitude," Mary assures me. "You'll get used to it."

"Yeah, babe, it's the altitude." He turns pale and avoids my gaze.

"Perry, what are you not telling me?"

When he finally looks at me, it's as if all of the oxygen has been sucked out of the room. The children are huddled over a large puzzle, their backs to us, and fear grips me.

"Ahh, I guess now's as good of a time as any. Babe? Remember that scan I had last year?"

"Of course I remember! You told me everything was okay . . . it was just a false positive!" I feel dizzy.

"Well . . . I had a decision to make—a fast one— and I know I should've let you in on it, but I was just so—"

"Perry! What have you done? What have we done?" I glance at our four signatures below the fine print on the last page. From the corner of my eye, I see Mary slip from the room, and I wonder why my heart's not beating furiously. Can a person be so frightened that all sensations cease?

"This way, we'll be together forever, just like we pledged on our wedding day!" Perry smiles, and my vision threatens to trick me again. I seem to see right through him.

"What? What do you mean? Perry? What's happening to you? What's happening to me?" I look at my hands and they fade from sight. I reach to touch Perry's cheek, and my hand passes through him. "Perry!"

"It's all right, babe. You'll get used to it, I promise."

"But, the children!" I look at them and they turn toward us with their suddenly pale faces. They stare at us with fleeting expressions of understanding, smile unearthly smiles, Rapheal takes Angela's wispy hand, and they float off to play with hosts of ethereal new friends who've just appeared from nowhere outside the office.

"See?" Perry startles me from my astonishment. "They've already adapted. You will, too. I promise. Let's go home now, babe."

He takes my hand somehow and we float through the office window. I look behind at the bodies of a lovely young family—husband and wife slumped in office chairs, two children in a corner collapsed over an unfinished puzzle.

As darkness falls in our new neighborhood, others like us rise from stony yards Dand float by to greet us. The old miner tips his hat and waves. Despite the holiday, the whole town seems quiet tonight.

When we drift inside our new home, I don't feel the cold anymore. I don't feel anything at all.

Huh. Perry's right. I'm already adapting. Guess I'll sleep like the dead tonight.

Tricky treat, indeed, my little angel.

15: CROW-MAGNUM

RUBY AND JADE SAT in their pink 1959 El Dorado convertible at a T-intersection in the middle of nowhere for several moments, both staring right, and then left, and then right again before looking at one another. There was nothing familiar about the rolling hills to the right or the winding road to the left, and there was nothing to see through the thick trees to their front.

"Well, this is depressing." Ruby released her grasp on the steering wheel. The twins were lost, the battery on their shared cell phone having died on their way home from a spelunking adventure.

"I've never seen a sky so gray. What do you think? Left or right?" Jade looked at their cell phone one last time before stashing it in the console. "I say we toss a coin. Anything to get away from this Texas Chainsaw Massacre vibe."

If they'd been city girls or scary movie fans, the whirr of a chainsaw in the distance might have frightened them.

"Don't worry, little sister, I know how to handle that .357." Ruby was grateful that their father, John, had taught them how to wield even the most temperamental of power tools and how to handle the .357 Magnum revolver they carried in their glove compartment.

"Little sister!" Jade scoffed. "What am I, like 30 seconds younger than you?"

"Hey, I clearly learned a lot in those 30 seconds! But look!" Ruby pointed to a crow flying high above them. It circled and disappeared.

"Weird, right?" Jade squinted into the dreary sky. The day was muggy and warm, and the open convertible top did little to cool the sweat from their bodies. "So, come on. You're the decisive one, *big* sister. Pick a direction!"

"I don't know. Neither one feels right. A GPS would've been handy. Not that there's any service out here. Can't believe we're still driving this old Bazooka on wheels. We're so *not* pink-car girls." Ruby smacked the dashboard, and immediately felt guilty.

Their father had purchased the car two years earlier for their 18th birthday, shortly after their mother had died of "natural causes." Twenty now, the girls routinely laughed at their father's gaffe.

"Hey! Go easy on her, *Ellie May*!"

"Really, Jade? It's bad enough when those horny teenagers call me that!" Ruby flicked a mosquito off her arm.

"I know. Sorry. *Daisy Duke* and *Ellie May*. I don't get it. We don't even dress like those hillbillies."

"It's the identical twin thing. Every guy's fantasy, right? You know you've felt it since we were kids. And the car doesn't help. I know dad meant well, but if he knew the shit we keep getting from guys—"

"It'd break his heart. We'll never be able to trade it in for something more—"

"Us? Yeah, I know." Ruby smoothed her hand across the dash. As they often did, the girls seamlessly finished the other's thoughts.

Not every pair of twins shared a psychic connection, but Ruby and Jade did.

"Arrg!" Jade threw her head back and ruffled her raven-colored hair, scanning the flat gray sky. "That chainsaw's getting on my nerves."

"Wait! There it is again!" Ruby looked up at the crow, which greeted them with a cacophonous caw this time.

"She's been following us since we left the cave," said Jade. "Do you think it's the same one that was—"

"Hanging around Mom's window for days before she died?" Ruby never minced words. "I think so. And so do you." She scratched where the mosquito had bitten.

"Yeah. Something about the sound it makes." Jade giggled. "Sounds like Mom, scolding us for getting lost. *'You should have listened to your father and taken a paper map, just in case!'*"

Ruby laughed at her sister's impersonation. "She was about as old fashioned as Dad, right? A paper map! But I really thought you had the backup charger for our phone."

"And I thought *you* had it. You think maybe we're old enough to have our own phones yet?"

"I dunno. It's not like you're ever that far from me." Ruby looked at her sister and smiled. She wouldn't admit it, but she felt more balanced when she was with Jade. More grounded.

"Oh, and now you sound just like Mom." Jade poked Ruby in the arm. "I'll give her credit, though. She sure could stretch a meal."

"And find a bargain. How she had the patience to sort through those thrift store racks, I'll never know." Ruby examined her clothes, smudged with dirt from the cave.

"She could sniff out the designers, too! Remember those Michael Kors jeans? They still had tags on them." Jade pouted. "Still bugs me they couldn't say why she died. It makes no sense, right? Do you ever even remember her being sick? You know, before she—"

"No." Ruby rubbed goosebumps from her brown arms and watched the crow circle overhead. She wasn't in any mood to discuss her mother's death. She often had to catch herself after grabbing the phone to text a message or a photo. She could still hear her mother's laughter.

Aiyana's death remained a mystery. None of the specialists could understand how she had gone from full vitality to a relentless decline over several months until her final day.

"And I'm worried about Dad. Doesn't seem like he wants to move on." Jade frowned.

"It's only been two years. Two years of us taking shit for driving this ridiculous car!" Ruby tried to lighten the mood, but to no avail.

The crow continued to circle overhead.

"Maybe you should kill the engine till our friend makes up her mind," Jade suggested. "I know we're going to end up following her. We can wait, but let's not run out of gas too."

"Good point." Ruby pulled off the road and killed the engine. "Hey, the cave was pretty cool, right? Be a great place to hide a body. They should make a Sherlock Holmes episode there."

"Wouldn't you just love to imagine your Benedict Cumber-crush filming nearby?" Jade taunted her sister.

"*You're* the one with a hard-on for him!" Ruby shoved her sister's arm, happy to be talking about anything other than their sorrow.

"Eeeww! That's just wrong! But yes. He's yummy. We'll share him. I wouldn't mind making *that* guy's fantasy come true!"

"Wow! You're bad," Ruby laughed, glancing at the undecided crow. "Let's play 'what if' while Rava makes up her mind."

"Rava?"

"Why not? Might as well give her a name if she's going to be hanging out with us."

"There's something odd about this crow. Do you feel it?" Jade asked. "It's not a bad feeling, but it's not exactly good, either."

"Yeah. It's just . . . different. Let's play." Ruby fidgeted in her seat.

"Okay. I'll start," said Jade. "What if we accidentally ate THC-laced brownies at a party?"

"Huh. Maybe we should try it sometime. What if we could fly just by thinking about it?" Ruby closed her eyes to imagine flying over the earth.

"That'd be awesome. We could be like Superman. No, Wonder Woman. We'll be protectors of the planet! You can keep the red bustier. Mine'll be green. We'll be Wonder Women! Okay. What if we were kidnapped and knew there was no way we'd ever escape or be rescued, even by our bootylicious Benedict?"

"Oh! Come on, now, you know he'd come to our rescue! Here's a good one. What if Dad isn't our real father?" Ruby glanced at the still-circling crow.

"Well, I guess that would explain his choice in cars! But, if he isn't our father, then who could be? Let's not go there! What if we went blind?"

"Then we wouldn't have to drive this relic anymore! Ha!" Ruby smacked the steering wheel and sighed. She saw Jade raise an eyebrow, waiting for the next 'what if.' "What if . . . what if someone killed Mom?"

Jade's jaw dropped. "Not possible. She was a saint! Everyone said so! You're not asking that seriously, are you?"

"I don't know. It's just that—"

"No. I can't even imagine. Just stop." Jade crossed her arms. "No more 'what ifs.' And OH—MY—GOD will that chainsaw ever stop?"

"I know, right? Feels like we're in a dentist office, doesn't it?" Ruby laughed joylessly. "I can almost smell burning tooth dust."

"Oh! Gross! Stop it! As if this isn't creepy enough." Jade shivered.

"I'd close the rooftop, but the breeze feels good."

"Whatever. I know you just want to watch Rava. And yeah, this is almost as bad as waiting for the drill. Remember Conroy's horrible hygienist, Clara?"

"*Clara, the Horrible Hygienist*! That'd make a great Stephen King children's book! How could I forget her?" Ruby chuckled. "The Marquis de Sade was probably her great-grandfather. And her breath! Holy shit!"

"No, just shit. Nothing holy about that snorting gum-gouger. Must've been embarrassing for Dad when he told Conroy we'd be switching dentists, but thank God Mom insisted."

"*There's a lesson for you girls,*" Ruby mimicked her father, "*never mix business with friendship.*"

"At least he kept bringing over free toothpaste samples!" Jade picked at something between her teeth.

"Yeah. We got all the fun flavors. And Mom always wanted '*only the least expensive brand, please.*' She was even frugal with free stuff! Dad never used what he gave us. And he probably still feels guilty over leaving Conroy's practice."

Both girls glanced at the crow.

"Why do you think Conroy and Ellen moved after Mom died?" Jade's voice was a whisper. "It's not like Conroy got a new job, and I heard their new place isn't much different."

"I don't know. Mom and Ellen were besties since we were little. Maybe it was too hard for her." Ruby frowned, angry at herself for having brought the conversation back to their mother.

"Too hard for *her*? What about Dad?" Jade crossed her arms again. "He was their friend too, and they abandoned him. They abandoned us. What kind of friend does that?"

"I don't know. Guess I'm just trying to come up with an excuse that makes sense." Ruby's brow furrowed as an old memory resurfaced. "Hey, remember those photos I showed you of Mom and Dad's anniversary a while ago?"

"The ones with Ellen looking like she had a fake smile? Didn't we decide she was probably having one of her infamous gas attacks from visiting the cheese platter too many times?"

Ruby laughed. "Yeah, those. Remember I also said I thought the way Conroy was looking at Mom seemed a bit . . . I don't know . . . more than just friendly?"

"And I told you to stop being such an amateur sleuth. Don't go there, Ruby. That's just gross. He was our science tutor, for God's sake, and Ellen edited our English papers. They've known us since we were what, five? They're practically . . . they *were* practically our aunt and uncle." Jade scrunched her lips together.

The crow startled them from their funk with another loud caw before descending toward them in a gentle spiral. They watched in awe as it landed on the hood of their El Dorado. Its shiny blackness contrasted stunningly against the pink paint and its sharp claws clip-clopped tentatively as it marched in a circle. The crow released another cry into the flat gray sky. Soon, another crow answered and joined the first. Ruby and Jade looked from the birds to one another and back to the birds again, their eyebrows raised in disbelief.

"Looks like Rava was just waiting for her friend," said Ruby.

The two birds hopped to the top edge of the windshield and stared into the twins' eyes. Mesmerized, they stared back, and time seemed to stand still.

"Ahhh, are you feeling what I'm feeling?" Jade asked.

"Yeah, and are you seeing what I'm seeing? Are their eyes glowing?"

"Yup. And growing?"

"Uh-huh!" Ruby leaned forward, her eyes locked on those of the bird in front of her. "It feels like I'm falling into her eyes. Did we eat something wacky back at the cave?"

"No, I don't think so." Jade stared into the new crow's eyes. "Should we let them do what I think they're asking?"

"Well, if you want me to make this decision too, I'll say yes. This is just so . . . weird and exciting, right?"

"Yup. I'm not afraid. Go for it, Shadow."

"Did she just tell you her name?" asked Ruby, still mesmerized by her crow.

"Yup. I heard it, or felt it, or something."

A moment later, the girls felt a tickling flutter of feathers on their cheeks as the birds lit atop their heads.

"Ahh . . .," Ruby looked at her sister, "their claws kinda feel like those wiry head massager thingies sold '*Only on TV*,' am I right?"

"Uh-huh. Wait a minute. They stopped moving."

"Whoa!" Ruby's eyes grew wide. "Who's that? Are you seeing this? It's like I'm looking through a fuzzy tunnel! What the—"

"If you're seeing a dude in a baseball cap, then yeah. He's locking the outside door of some office building. I can't see his face, though, can you? And . . . Ruby . . . what the fuck?"

"I don't know! He's putting a gym bag into his trunk. Go ahead and call me an amateur sleuth, but the dude looks like he's sneaking around. Like he's hiding something."

"No, I agree. He's driving off now."

The crows disengaged abruptly and hopped back onto the top edge of the windshield.

"What just happened?" Both girls asked simultaneously before looking back at the crows.

"Not sure," said Ruby, "but . . . and don't ask me how or why, but I think they're trying to tell us something."

The crows gazed into the girls' eyes one more time before taking flight and soaring side by side down the hill to their left. Ruby knew this was her cue to follow. She finally had a direction to turn, even if the decision had been made by crows.

"Good riddance, chainsaw." Ruby started the engine, pulled onto the road, and turned left. A brilliant beam of setting sunlight broke through the overcast ahead of them, briefly illuminating the birds. "I'll take that as a good sign. Let's see where they'll take us, shall we, Watson?"

"Oh, so I'm the sidekick?" Jade asked.

"But of course! If you recall, you're the one who volunteered to wear the *green* bustier!"

"Yeah, okay, guilty as charged." Jade chuckled, and then murmured, "Doc's more sensible anyway."

The girls were quiet for a while as they followed the crows, which were never out of sight.

"Look! I recognize that road," Ruby said, turning on her blinker. "I know the way home from here." She relaxed her shoulders.

But the birds remained on a straight path beyond the turnoff.

"I know you're ready to go home, but—"

"But they're taking us somewhere else, right?" Ruby finished Jade's thought. "Are you up for it, or are we just being stupid?" She would trust Jade's judgement.

"Let's keep following. At least until we have to refuel. If we have to stop and they keep flying away, then maybe we're just being silly because we're overtired. Deal?"

"Deal. They're trying to show us something. I have no idea how or why, but I just know it, and I know you feel it too."

Jade nodded, her eyes locked onto the mysterious crows.

Ruby wouldn't say it, but she believed the crows' appearance had something to do with their mother.

Several miles beyond the turnoff Ruby had hoped to take, the crows flew toward the next town beyond their own. It was the town where Ellen and Conroy had moved, though they'd never invited their old friends to visit. Twenty minutes later, the crows slowed and circled over the top of a house at the end of a long, sparsely populated road.

"Isn't that the car we saw in our vision?" Jade whispered, though there was no one around to hear her but her sister.

"Yeah. Hey, it's getting dark, but these wheels'll stand out like a six-foot tall redhead in China. Let's park farther down the street and see what's up."

The birds seemed to approve of their decision. They landed on the hood of the car again and hopped to the top of the windshield. When they locked eyes with the girls as they had before, Ruby and Jade knew what was coming next: a flutter of feathers and a perch upon their heads. This time, the visions they relayed were horrifying.

"Oh, shit!" Ruby whispered.

Like Odin's ravens Huginn and Muninn, the crows relayed the thoughts and memories of the man in the house to the twins. But instead of by whispers, they communicated via their claws, spread through the girls' thick black hair and strategically anchored onto specific spots.

"It's Conroy. He looks pissed," said Jade.

Their old neighbor was alone, and pouring himself a generous double of Jameson. He picked up a photo of his wife from his fireplace mantle and smashed it into an open fireplace.

"You think you can just leave me?" he screamed at the cold bricks. "You're just like all of them. You just wait. I'll find a way to get you like I got Aiyana."

The girls both gasped and grabbed hands, startling the crows from the perch on their heads and back onto the windshield where they waited for the girls to settle down. They waited for many minutes while Ruby and Jade stared at one another before bursting into hushed discussion about the brief vision.

"What the fuck, Jade! I told you something wasn't right about him!"

"But . . . but . . . Conroy? What did he do? Ellen left him? I don't understand!" There were tears in Jade's eyes.

Without answering her sister, Ruby turned back to the birds. "Show us more," she demanded, "and Jade, you need to stay calm, understand?"

Jade nodded and wiped her eyes, and the birds returned atop the girls' heads—Rava on Ruby's, Shadow on Jade's.

The next vision was from Conroy's memory, and the girls could see their mother through the man's eyes—his longing, fantasizing eyes. They could hear his internal dialogue.

"Why did she pick him? What could I have done to make her realize she should be with me—that she should leave that lowlife scum? What's wrong with me, or is she like all the others—thinking she's too good for me? Me, a successful doctor! But she stays with that sweaty ranch hand instead. Makes no sense. Didn't she notice my glances? Didn't she feel the electricity whenever I touched her? Didn't I show up whenever she needed a favor? Well, if I can't have her—"

"Oh my God," Ruby whispered, "he's deranged."

They watched as Conroy formulated his plan years earlier when he finally accepted Aiyana would not leave her husband and run away with him. It was a simple, brilliant plan. All he had to do was add a little something to the tube of cheap toothpaste he routinely delivered with a smile along with the others. Aiyana was the only one in the household who used that formula, so there'd be no chance of harming the girls.

Conroy's inner thoughts continued. *"Hurting the twins would be wrong. They're still too young to break a man's heart."*

"The toothpaste," Jade whispered, her eyelids fluttering in the vision as it continued.

Once Conroy had the toothpaste tube crimper, the rest was easy. He'd start by adding just a bit of his concoction to the paste, and once Aiyana started exhibiting signs of illness, he'd increase the amount slowly with each new tube. No one would think to test for his newly fabricated chemical, and she'd eventually succumb to the poison.

The girls were suddenly in Conroy's head at their mother's funeral.

"Good job, ol' boy! Brilliant as always! Too bad the bitch wasn't smart enough to see how much better her life would have been with me."

And then the man's thoughts jumped to the present.

"We have to stop him!" Jade whispered. "He's planning to find Ellen and—"

"Kill her," Ruby finished. "He thinks she's going to go to the police. He's going to kill her and leave the country. He's going to keep killing, Jade. He's sick."

Still experiencing visions from the crows, the girls watched Conroy pace back and forth in front of his fireplace, babbling to himself.

"Yeah, a nice long vacation," he said. "Plenty of other stupid women in relationships with mediocre men. I'll relieve them of their burdensome lives. I'll take my time. No one'll ever find out."

But the crows knew what he'd done. And so, now, did the girls. What the birds planted in their minds was startling. It was also thrilling. A new kind of justice was being offered.

"We need to make a decision, Jade."

"You make it," Jade whispered. "I'll do whatever you decide."

"No. We make this one together. Yes or no, on the count of three. One . . . two . . ."

On the count of three, both girls whispered "Yes."

There was no time to question why the crows had waited more than two years to show them the truth—Conroy was readying himself to leave his house. Perhaps the birds knew the girls had needed time to mature and harden their emotions. Perhaps they wanted to ensure the girls were up for the responsibilities ahead, the ones that would follow this grim task. It didn't matter. Rava and Shadow made it clear to the girls that they were at a turning point in their lives.

The crows disengaged and flew to the hood of the car.

"We could still drive away, right now," Ruby offered. "We could raise this wonky roof and drive away, go get a pizza and pretend this never happened. We could go home, recharge this stupid phone, and help Dad set up a dating profile."

"Or we can do what Shadow and Rava are suggesting. Do we really have a choice, Ruby? Can you let Mom's murderer walk free, knowing he's already planning to kill again?"

"We could call the police—"

"And say what? Even if we could call them, which we can't, there's no way they'll believe our story. They'll want answers. They'll want to know how we knew about Conroy. And what'll we say? 'Oh, well, you see, officers, these two crows told us everything.' They'll lock *us* up!"

"Okay, okay. But we wait till he comes outside, right? And then . . . and then . . ."

Jade opened the glove compartment, checked the cylinder of the .357 to ensure it was loaded, and handed the gun to her sister. "You have the steadier hand," she said, as if they'd practiced this drill countless times before.

The crows watched from the top of the windshield. Both girls got out of the car and took slow steps toward the house. Ruby let the handgun hang by her side. Beads of sweat gathered on her foreheads and under her arms.

"We've only practiced at the range, Jade. What if I can't do it?"

"Conroy poisoned Mom."

"Right. Right. Shit! He's opening his door! Stay near me, Jade."

"I'm right here. We can do this."

The girls stopped at the end of Conroy's driveway and waited for him to see them. When he did, he jumped back, nearly tumbled over a shrub, and let out a high-pitched exclamation. He squinted in the darkness toward them, and when it was clear he recognized them, he opened his arms to them.

"What a lovely surprise! I've been meaning to invite you over, but—"

He dropped his arms when Ruby raised hers.

"We know what you did, you sonovabitch," Jade said.

"Why? Why'd you do it, Conroy? We were your friends! We treated you like family!" Ruby kept the weapon pointed at that man, whose hands were held out in front of him, as if they could stop a bullet.

"Oh, now, surely you couldn't pull the trigger on an old friend! You're not a murderer! Look! I'll go to the police first thing in the morning and turn myself in, I swear. There's just something very important I need to do tonight. Put down the gun, girl. I'm an important man, you know. I'll do the right thing. You do the right thing too."

For a moment, Ruby waivered. He had a point. She wasn't a murderer. And could she truly pull the trigger on an old friend? But just as she was lowering her weapon, Rava settled back onto her head and showed her the thoughts streaming through Conroy's mind in real time. He was laughing inside. He knew neither of the twins could harm him.

"You're stupid, scared girls," he was thinking. *"I can see it on your faces and in the dark sweat stains on your shirts. I'll send you home believing my promise, I'll carry out my plan for Ellen, and be on the next flight to the Netherlands. You're just stupid girls, as stupid as your mother was."*

Ruby raised her weapon again; it would be an easy shot to the heart at less than 20 feet. Could she kill him? Of course she could. This was not some kindly old neighbor. This was a deceptive, evil man who'd planned and executed a brilliant murder without regard for the other lives he'd destroyed or remorse for what he'd done.

Conroy appeared ready to bolt, and as Ruby moved her finger onto the trigger, the crow stopped her with a vision and an offer. Yes, she could pull the trigger—she had made the decision, was ready to, and wanted to. But the crow's plan was stunning.

"Jade, send Shadow, now!"

Jade looked at her crow and, in an unwavering voice, said, "Fire when ready." Instantly, Shadow flew toward Conroy, threatening him from above with a raucous caw that sounded more to the girls like *kill*.

"What the hell?" Conroy yelled, raising his arms to bat the bird away, and Rava disengaged from Ruby's head.

As Conroy struggled to fend off Shadow, the girls watched as Rava flew high into the darkening sky until she nearly disappeared before returning like a missile. Just before impacting the place Ruby's bullet would have pierced, Rava's black beak lengthened into a razor-sharp point and her feathers transformed into segmented, articulating armor, spreading down to protect her body just before impact.

The expression on Conroy's face before he hit the ground was one the girls would never forget—it was an expression of disgust, contempt, and utter disbelief.

The following morning, Conroy's mail deliverer called the police after seeing the man on the ground. He was at a loss for how to describe the man's wound.

"It looks like there's, ah, a really big hole through his heart from front to back," he said, his voice trembling.

When the police and coroner arrived, they too were confused.

"Look here," the coroner pointed. "Crow tail feathers on the ground. And there's one stuck to this shattered rib. Odd."

"Been a lot of crows in town this year," said a police officer, as if that explained anything.

"Over here!" another officer called from the back of Conroy's vehicle. He pulled out several vials of mysterious liquid and an abundance of travel-size toothpaste tubes from a gym bag in Conroy's trunk. "Better get these to the lab."

The twins woke to a hubbub in their front yard. Reporters had gotten wind of a story connecting the dead dentist to John's family.

"We tell him nothing, Jade. Just that the cave was awesome and we stayed longer than we'd planned."

Jade nodded. "Ah, Dad?" she knocked on her father's bedroom door. "We heard something on the radio this morning. You might want to come out here."

"Something about Conroy," Ruby added, talking loudly through the door. "The police want to talk with anyone who's been his patient, and there are reporters outside. We're heading out now. You might want to put on pants."

They went to the back door, and as they opened it, a realization hit them at the same time, as it often had in the past. Ruby spoke first.

"He's not the last vicious criminal out there, you know."

"We should stay in school, though. We'll need a cover."

"We're really doing this, then? You're with me? Because I don't think I can to this without you, little sister."

Jade nodded.

"This is no game, Jade. This means we're hunters now—and not for meals."

"I know." Jade faced Ruby and took her sister's hands into her own.

A sudden ruckus from the reporters startled them. Their father had opened the front door.

"And we can't tell anyone." Ruby's voice was hushed, but intense. "Our lives won't be easy. And it won't be like your Wonder Women fantasy—we don't have superpowers."

"No, but for whatever reason, we do have something special."

"We'll be taking justice into our own hands. We could get caught. They could lock us up, and then what would happen to Dad?"

"We won't let that happen, Ruby. Rava and Shadow won't let that happen. You felt it last night, didn't you? That we'd be safe? That we were meant to be there?"

Ruby nodded. She had felt it. She gave her sister a bear hug and the two snuck out the back door.

Avoiding the crowd at the front of their house, they made their way to the pink El Dorado and buckled up.

"I wonder when we'll get our next mission," said Ruby. "Seems we made it to Conroy's place just in time."

"We avenged Mom's murder last night, Ruby. Damn. It's just hitting me now." Jade squeezed her eyes closed, but not before tears fell.

Ruby wondered why she hadn't been able to cry yet. She looked up to see Rava soaring in a slow circle overhead before landing on the hood of the car. Shadow followed closely behind.

"Where to next, girls?" Ruby asked. No time for tears today.

Rava squawked, and then she and Shadow flew north.

Jade wiped her eyes, tied her hair back into a neat ponytail, and said, "Let's do this."

"Yeah. Let's. And what do you say we name this ol' car?"

"I'd say that's the best idea you've had today!"

With a full charge on their cell phone and a paper map under their seat, the twins drove north toward their next unknown encounter. They'd made a decision to dole out a new kind of justice in a world controlled by those who thought they were too clever to get caught after committing heinous crimes against innocents.

Their adventures had just begun.

* This is the first episode of **Crow-Magnum**. Artist Becky Jewell is creating graphic novels based on this new series . . . watch for them!

16: THE FOXHOLE

"SO, WHAT DO YOU have planned for me this afternoon?" Michelle's face scrunched involuntarily as she downed the last dregs of her coffee, black. "And when are you gonna get a *real* coffee maker?"

"Hey, there's nothing realer than a percolator. And don't think you'll be seeing any Keurigs where you're going, young lady." Michelle's mother, Lynn, took the empty cup and set it in the sink next to her own. "Let's finish up the foxhole, and then there's another project that shouldn't take too long."

"Are you sure you're up to going today, Mom?"

"Never been more sure of anything in my life."

"But you always say that! Are you ever *not* sure about anything?"

Her mother smiled. "I'm not sure. Let me think about that. Ah . . . no, I'm sure."

Michelle shoved her mother gently, then wrapped her arms around her. "I'm the only girl I know whose mother is making her dig a foxhole. But I'm worried about you, you know."

"I know, Chelle. No need, though. Come on, enough lollygagging. It's a perfect day and we're not getting any younger. And you might be the only girl you know who can dig a foxhole better than any other newbie at The Academy."

The two women strolled side-by-side, bumping against one another occasionally as if drawn together by a magnetic bond. The land spread out before them, Colorado wildflower season in full bloom, and their destination was a quarter mile from their home.

"Have you ever regretted going to West Point? I mean, I've heard your stories, but it must've been crazy hard back then."

"Crazy hard, yes, but no regrets. I don't believe in regrets. As your dad's hero, Teddy, once said, nothing's worth having or doing unless there's effort, pain, and hardship involved. Something like that. I say, make a decision and own it. Don't look back and wish you'd done something different—you didn't, so move forward. And it's not like it's going to be a cakewalk for you this year."

"I know, but you're right. Pretty sure I'll be a lot more prepared than most of my classmates." Michelle stopped. "Wow. How lucky are we to have all this land!" She turned in a slow circle. "Mount Elbert over there, Turquoise Lake over there, there's not a bad view anywhere."

"Our ancestors were no dummies. It'll be yours someday." Lynn took a deep breath, a simple act that had grown harder to do over the past several months. She put on a smile before Michelle completed her loop. "So many Columbines this year! Would you pick me a bunch of those paintbrushes, hun? Some daisies, too."

Another deep breath.

With modest bouquets in hand, they continued their trek.

"Men will hit on you, Chelle."

"Mom! Come on! As if you haven't prepared me for that too." Michelle rolled her eyes. "You and Dad have been running me through self-defense moves since I was what? Five?"

They laughed.

"Really, though. And it won't matter what rank you are or what rank they are."

"Enough already! You taught me well. You don't have to worry about me. Any guy stupid enough to try pushing something on me is gonna wish he'd left his junk in a trunk."

"Good. And there'll be times you'll be told to do things that seem wrong to you, but unless your orders are illegal or immoral, you'll have to put on your big girl panties and say, 'Yes, ma'am.' There'll be gray areas, of course."

"I've heard *everything* at West Point is a gray area!" Michelle raised an eyebrow.

"Very punny," said Lynn. "Keep your sense of humor, and you'll be okay. Trust your good judgment. My grampa used to say, 'Don't let the bastards get you down.'"

"Why all the lessons today? I don't leave for another whole month!"

"Just making sure I've covered all the bases. Oh, and my father's advice was, 'Keep your mouth shut and your bowels open,' something his father suggested before he shipped off to World War II."

"Gross, Mom! Thanks for that disturbing visual."

"Trust me, it's good advice! You go on ahead. I'll be right there."

Michelle handed her flowers to her mother and ran the rest of the way to the nearly completed foxhole. When she got there, she bent over to pick up several sheets of paper from a stack of wooden planks. "Seriously, Mom?" she shouted. "An Ikea bench? Are you trying to break up with me?"

Lynn smiled and continued to stroll, taking in the beauty of the landscape. When she reached the foxhole, she laid the flowers on one of the wooden planks and joined her daughter, who was studying the cartoon drawings in the step-by-step assembly instructions.

Michelle laughed and pointed to one. "Check it out! This one actually shows the dude reading the instruction manual with a frowny face and then picking up a phone! And what does that one even mean?"

"I think it means, don't look at the jumbled pile of wood alone, be confused with a friend!" Lynn flipped to the next page.

"And you obviously have to be a man to put this together. I don't know, Mom," Michelle affected a southern drawl, "it's just us two li'l ol' girls here. However will we survive this big ol' construction project?"

Lynn smiled, but was glad her daughter was too engrossed in the instructions to notice the sorrow in her smile, or to question the quantity of wood delivered for the project.

Michelle jumped into the foxhole and picked up a shovel. "I'm thinking this is pretty much done, wouldn't you agree? Six'ish feet long, about three feet wide, and if we scrunch down, it's good enough for government work." She rested her arms on the ground outside the hole and looked out across the panorama. "Now I see why the bench. Why didn't we put one here before?"

"Just wasn't the right time, I suppose." Lynn examined the hole. "Give me three more inches depth, soldier! And no sniveling!"

"Yes, ma'am!" Michelle saluted her mother and started digging. "How about if you start on the bench while I'm down here so we'll have time to sit on it before sunset?"

"Yes, ma'am back atcha!" Lynn returned her daughter's salute and started sorting the planks. It was slow work. She assembled all but the back rest and stopped when the dizziness struck and her vision blurred.

Time passed.

"That's good, Chelle. Come on out now." Lynn sat on the bench and patted the spot next to her for Michelle to sit.

Michelle climbed from the hole and looked at the remaining wooden planks, two of which were cut differently than the others. She looked at her mother. She didn't sit. Her chin quivered.

"Mom?"

"It's time, Chelle. Your father knows. Please, sit with me."

"But—"

"No buts, my beautiful girl. You're going to have to be stronger than ever now, for what's ahead of you and for your father."

"But—" Michelle looked again at the finished foxhole and at the panels of wood still remaining, wood she originally assumed would be used over the foxhole for concealment. "But you're—"

"I'm giving you a gift. I'm giving your father a gift. I'm giving . . . myself this gift."

Michelle fell onto the bench at her mother's side and wept in her arms. Lynn rocked her daughter gently with what little strength remained in her failing body.

"And if I learn that you're thinking about quitting," Lynn whispered in a voice threatening to crack, "or that you've let some asshole make you cry, I swear I'll haunt you."

"Promise?" Michelle laughed through her tears.

"Promise. Momma didn't raise no butterfly, did she?"

"No, Momma." Michelle sat up and wiped her eyes with her dirty hands, leaving muddy streaks across her face.

The two women sat silently then, their sides locked together—looking out over the foxhole, over the wilting bouquets waiting on a pallet, across to the shimmering lake—until the sun disappeared behind the mountain range.

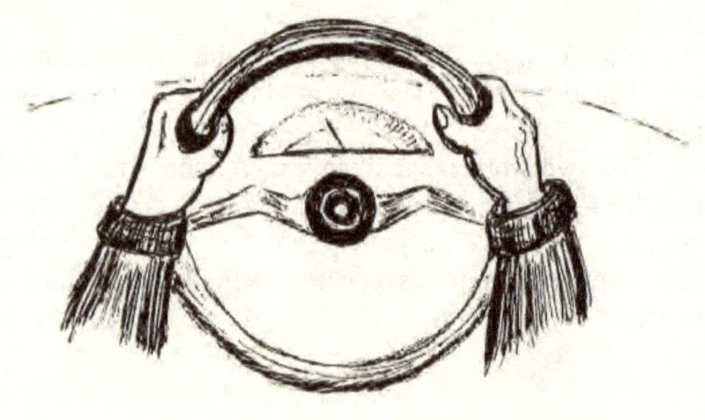

17: PEARL AT THE WHEEL

"YOU LOOK COLD, dear." Pearl pushed her jacket onto Frank's lap, keeping her eyes on the road. It was her turn to drive the '58 Oldsmobile coupe, Frank's pride and joy, second only to his wife.

Frank's proposal nearly 65 years earlier had made her giggle.

"Please be my forever girl, my lovely Pearl! I'll do my best never to irritate you!"

Pearl had cherished each day since becoming Mrs. Frank Newhart. Her husband had a way of making everything wonderful, even the childless years when she had questioned why he would keep her as a wife.

" 'Twasn't meant for you to take care of anyone but me, my bumblebee! You know you're my whole worl', Pearl. Now, give me a hug."

And with each hug she knew her place in his heart was safe.

She was uneasy behind the wheel of "Ol' Brownie," but Frank had already driven through the morning and she could tell he was weary. They drove only during daylight hours now that their vision wasn't the best. Their last drive south had been hairy, and Frank's frequent remarks about the "daredevil whippersnappers" on the road had made her reconsider this year's trip.

"Oh, but the kids'll miss us! We'll just take it slow. What do you say? Shall we give it another whirl, my pretty Pearl? Just one more jaunt?"

Pearl could never say no to her Frank. Even when his plans involved doing things she'd never imagined, she trusted he would keep her from harm and expand the small world of her past.

And he was patient. She never understood how he could be so patient with her fretful ways.

Frank was a good driver, too, and loved their road trips, but the journey to visit their favorite nephew's family took days. There was no need to hurry in either direction, though, so she helped him pack the car.

" 'Twill be an adventure, my tweety-sweetie-pie," he told her.

"It's always an adventure with you, dear. But I think we'll fly next time."

They had just passed the "WELCOME TO OKLAHOMA: Discover the Excellence" sign when she stole a glance at her husband. How she loved his strong nose, his wispy silver hair, his bushy eyebrows, and the mischievous grin that always played around his lips.

"How can you tell if he's happy or sad?" their friends would ask her because his expression never seemed to change, even when Pearl knew he was troubled. She wondered if it was his way of protecting her fragile emotions.

"Oh, I know," was all she'd say.

Pearl grasped the wheel and briefly considered pulling over to the shoulder. "These double-long trucks scare the bejeebers out of me. Look at him! He's taking up half our lane! They should be illegal. Hey! You! Pick a lane! Should be illegal, don't you think?"

Jittery chatter was how Pearl dealt with tense situations. She drove on more slowly, her knuckles white at ten and two.

Another quick glance at Frank reminded her how patient he'd been over the years. When he learned she'd be fine once she finished her rant, he'd wait it out, the little furrows on either side of his mouth indicating an ever-present grin like the one he wore now.

"I sure will be glad to see that 'Welcome to Colorful Colorado' sign. Tomorrow, maybe. Isn't it just the funniest? Cream letters on a brown sign. Colorful Colorado. Ha!" She squinted. "This is the worst time to drive, you know, with the sun setting. Maybe we'll drive through the night tonight. Get home in time for Bridge with the girls tomorrow. Won't they be jealous when I tell them about the show at The Grand Ole Opry?"

When the truck was out of sight, she took a deep breath but didn't relax her grip on the wheel. She stared straight ahead, concentrating on keeping Ol' Brownie between her lane markers.

She let the silence sink in.

Miles later, Pearl placed her hand over Frank's.

"Still cold, darlin'?" She pulled her hand away quickly and fumbled to adjust the heat knob.

Tears threatened the corners of her eyes, rolled over her sparse lashes and disappeared in the soft scarf Frank had purchased that morning to protect her from Colorado's impending winter chill. She wiped the rest away brusquely. Wind buffeted the car and she grasped the wheel firmly again.

"I wish you'd say something, my love. Anything."

But Frank had nothing more to say. He had stopped talking near the eastern edge of Oklahoma shortly after their last McDonald's coffee when Pearl took over at the wheel.

There were two more states to traverse before they'd be home. She'd have to be careful where she stopped. Maybe she'd close his eyes and lean him against the door.

It would look like he was just sleeping.

NOTE: This short story was first published on November 21, 2016 and won a 2nd place award in ***Messages from the Hidden Lake, Vol 8: Literary & Art Collection of the Alamosa Public Library***

18: THE BLESSED BISCUIT

SAMUEL DIDN'T KNOW how his tie got stapled to the wall. Nor did he understand how he could have been transported, unaware, to this uncomfortable wooden chair facing the corner of his office, his expensive new Armani tie—ruined by industrial staple holes—binding him to this spot like a punished child, mocking him. What the hell had happened? Carol would be furious.

Marrying Carol, his high school sweetheart, had been the best decision Sam had ever made; but that was thousands of decisions ago. After several years of happiness together, despite many failed attempts to add a child to their home, Carol finally became pregnant.

Sarah was born to them on January 6th, Epiphany, their own little miracle baby.

One night, when Sarah was snuggled and silent and six-year-old, Sam asked Carol, "What do you think? Should I take it?"

"Well, it is a sizeable raise, and you've been looking for more responsibility. But it's also a competing bank. Your friends won't be too happy. And what about you?"

"It's not really about me. We have Sarah to think about now," he said, and that seemed to answer the question.

So, after many years as manager of his hometown bank, where he had enjoyed a sufficient salary, friendly work environment, and "banker's hours," he left his comfortable job for a higher level one that would pay better and allow him to provide more for his family.

"Anybody out there?" Sam yelled.

Silence.

Surveying his plush office, Sam wondered who could have pulled such a prank on him, and on Christmas Eve, of all times. He remembered the office party, if it could be called a party. Twenty-five overworked employees itching to get home after the mandatory sharing of holiday cheer. The company had even brought in a Santa—an amazingly authentic-looking one—in an ironic attempt to show how much the management cared about its people. But Sam couldn't seem to remember anything that happened after Santa had opened his gift bag.

Whoever had done this to him wanted to make sure he'd stay in this corner for a long time. The elaborately patterned tie was stapled countless times, both lengths of silk firmly attached in a way that prevented him from slipping it over his head or from simply pulling it away from the wall. He couldn't reach the scissors on his desk. Or the phone.

"Anybody? Roger?"

Roger was the night guard. Surely he'd be by soon. But time passed, and Roger never showed.

Perhaps it was best, he thought, that no one was around to witness what might have been a comical situation on any other day. But he could see the hands pointing to eleven o'clock. He had certainly missed reading Sarah her "Night Before Christmas" bedtime story.

Angry and ashamed, he began working to free himself.

Laboriously picking each staple from the wall, Sam questioned the decisions that brought him to this point— stuck, literally, in a high-priced office in a high-paying job with high-stress obligations. Friends and co-workers from his old bank had invited him to their holiday party days earlier, and the joyful atmosphere was real and personal.

Knowing full well his pay was half of what Sam's new employment paid, the interim manager had jokingly offered him his job back. Everyone had laughed, but there was no smile on Sam's face as he drove to work the following morning. He couldn't remember smiling since he'd first donned this ruined tie months ago.

Finally, with sore fingers and torn nails, Sam pulled back from his corner prison. He wondered how he would explain the damaged wall. It wasn't too bad, he thought, as he ran his fingers over the small holes. Then, startled by what looked like a pattern, he turned his head sideways and saw letters appear in the Braille-like bumps. He read them aloud, like a school child: "H," "A," "P," "Y."

The acronym meant nothing to him.

Tired, frustrated, and in no mood for games, Sam tossed the tie into the trashcan and made his way home. Carol would probably be asleep, he figured, and waking up to a joyful Christmas morning would override any lingering anger she might feel. All Sam really wanted to do was give his family the best he could. But right now, he wasn't sure what that meant.

The roads were empty. Everyone was already home, with visions of sugarplums dancing in their heads. He pulled into the garage and walked into a quiet kitchen, the aroma of tomorrow's pumpkin pie lingering in the air. It made him hungry.

On a child's table in the corner of the kitchen lay a crayon-smudged letter to Santa and a holiday plate upon which rested a homemade biscuit. He recognized the biscuit, an enormous monstrosity to behold, lovingly created days earlier with flour and water and egg and entirely too much salt, and baked just a bit too long. Sarah had made this especially for Santa in hopes of making her most desired Christmas wish come true.

Smiling, Sam picked up and read the childish scrawl:

> *Deer Santa, evin tho I Like to hav a new dol and a Tedy Beer, wat I wont MOOR is to hav my Daddy get his Old job bak. I don't tink he iz hapy now but he was hapy befor. And I was hapy to cuz I got lots moor hugs cus he waz home moor. If you eet my speshal biskit I wil no you wil giv him hiz Old job bak and I wil be hapy agin. You can shar my biskit with the deer if you wont. O and my Mum wonts a new kofee pot cuz I didn't meen to drop the old wun and* kan *you pleez giv my Daddy a new Ti? Luv Sarah*

The new doll and overstuffed teddy-bear were already conspicuously placed under the tree along with several other presents Carol and Sam knew Sarah would love. Sam had known about those items, the easy and obvious holiday hits. But he was completely unprepared to deliver what his daughter wanted most.

Or was he?

Sam looked at the small, uncomfortable, wooden child's chair in the corner, the note, the biscuit, and reflected on the corner he'd found himself trapped in just hours ago. It had been a long, stressful, bizarre day. The clock on the wall began to gong the countdown to Christmas morning.

A smile lit Sam's face. There was really nothing more for him to think about. Everything suddenly became clear. All that was left to do was sit down and eat that biscuit.

19: HER ONLY VICE

**[because I can't let you go without a
truly creepy story!]**

IT WAS HER ONLY VICE, really—her need for
stimulating conversation with young people. And the
city crawled with them.

"Twenty dollars to help an old lady with her
groceries?" She'd find a loner, and her offer never failed.
Once inside her end unit apartment, she'd sweeten the

deal. "Another Jackson to visit a bit? Tell me about your day? Here . . . I'll get you a nice drink."

One heavily spiked coke inevitably led to another, and often another. The relaxed teen, drunk on cheap rum, would relish spilling his sorrows to an attentive teetotaler.

"Tell me more! I'll make you famous. See? I'm writing a book." She'd flip through mounting ink-filled pages, and slurred stories would flow with more alcohol.

Eventually, she'd excuse herself to the powder room. Her startled scream of "Spider!"—perfectly pitched to provoke a groggy response from her guest— would position him just right, peering into her tub.

She was surprisingly strong for her age, though it didn't take much to push him in once she sliced his throat.

"That's a good boy," she'd say, holding him down as he flailed, briefly, futilely, and then, time for the real work.

Always frugal, she'd carefully preserve the juice, fitting each tender slice perfectly into vacuum-sealed packages. Her reward after stacking them in her freezer? Fresh liver and onions.

"She was the perfect neighbor," they'd say if she ever slipped up.

She was the perfectly innocuous little old lady.

ACKNOWLEDGMENTS

Mike McHargue, my ever-supportive and encouraging husband, thank you for being the greatest patron of my work. I never would have completed and published the number of books and podcast episodes I have out there in the world without your steadfast reassurance and belief that what I'm creating is far better than good! And thank you for convincing me to draw my own sketches for each chapter in this book. I love you.

To author Stephanie Spong, thank you for reading and approving this collection and offering insightful, constructive literary suggestions as you have with all my work to make my writing shine.

To John Orville Stewart, thank you for expressing surprise and appreciation for every story in this book.

To another author, I remain forever grateful for the years of encouragement, editing, tweaking and advice you've generously offered to improve my work.

To all of my Patreon supporters including top level patrons of my podcast *Alligator Preserves*—Joanne Bowman, Charlene McDade, Stephanie R. Sorensen, and Mary Wilson—thank you for supporting my creativity on air and helping to provide needed funding for the production costs of this book. I am eternally grateful to you.

To my parents, Pat and Charlie Bernier, who—even from beyond—continue to inspire characters, conversations, and ideas. I love and miss you.

ABOUT THE AUTHOR

Award-winning author Laurel McHargue, a 1983 West Point grad, lives and laughs and publishes and podcasts in Colorado's Rocky Mountains! Find her fantasy adventure trilogy *Waterwight* and other multi-genre works on Amazon, subscribe to her podcast *Alligator Preserves,* and sign up for her newsletter on her website to keep up with her latest appearances and publications.

www.laurelmchargue.com

~A FEW MORE WORDS FROM LAUREL~

I would love to hear from you!
Connect with me here:

Facebook: Leadville Laurel (author page)
Twitter: @LeadvilleLaurel
LinkedIn: Laurel (Bernier) McHargue
Web Page: www.laurelmchargue.com
Email: laurel@strackpress.com
Podcast: Alligator Preserves

Check out my other books on my **Amazon Author page** and let me know what you think!

And remember, we struggling authors/musicians/artists/actors love positive feedback, so if you like what we do, please consider writing reviews of our work! If you don't like what we do, well, if you can't say something nice . . .

:)

ALSO BY LAUREL MCHARGUE

Hai CLASS ku: Classroom Warm-ups

Haikus Can Amuse: 366 Haiku Starters

Hunt for Red Meat (love stories)

"Miss?"

The Hare, Raising Truth

Waterwight: Book I of the Waterwight Series

Waterwight Flux: Book II of the Waterwight Series

Waterwight Breathe: Book III of the Waterwight Series